W9-BYP-457

Hunting Houses

Hunting Houses

FANNY BRITT

Translated by Susan Ouriou
and Christelle Morelli

LUDINGTON
PUBLIC LIBRARY & INFORMATION CENTER
5 S. BRYN MAWR AVENUE
BRYN MAWR, PA 19010-3406

ARACHNIDE

Copyright © 2015 Le Cheval d'août
English translation copyright © 2017 Christelle Morelli and Susan Ouriou

First published as *Les maisons* in 2015 by Le Cheval d'août
First published in English in 2017 by House of Anansi Press Inc.
www.houseofanansi.com

All rights reserved. No part of this publication may be reproduced or transmitted in any
form or by any means, electronic or mechanical, including photocopying, recording, or any
information storage and retrieval system, without permission in writing from the publisher.

House of Anansi Press is committed to protecting our natural environment.
As part of our efforts, the interior of this book is printed on paper that contains 100% post-
consumer recycled fibres, is acid-free, and is processed chlorine-free.

21 20 19 18 17   1 2 3 4 5

Library and Archives Canada Cataloguing in Publication

Britt, Fanny, 1977-
[Maisons. English]
Hunting houses / Fanny Britt ; Susan Ouriou and Christelle Morelli, translators.

Translation of: Les maisons.
Issued in print and electronic formats.
ISBN 978-1-4870-0238-1 (softcover).--ISBN 978-1-4870-0239-8 (epub).—
ISBN 978-1-4870-0240-4 (Kindle)

I. Ouriou, Susan, translator II. Morelli, Christelle, translator
III. Title. IV. Title: Maisons. English.

PS8603.R5877M3513 2017   C843'.6   C2016-906687-8
                                           C2016-907021-2

Book design: Alysia Shewchuk

*We acknowledge for their financial support of our publishing program
the Canada Council for the Arts, the Ontario Arts Council, and the Government of Canada
through the Canada Book Fund. We acknowledge the financial support of the Government of
Canada, through the National Translation Program for Book Publishing, an initiative of the
Roadmap for Canada's Official Languages 2013–2018: Education, Immigration, Communities,
for our translation activities.*

Printed and bound in Canada

For Sam

Houses are cluttered with wishes,
the invisible furniture on which
we keep bruising our shins.
— Rebecca Solnit,
*The Encyclopedia of Trouble
and Spaciousness*

His House

I DON'T YET KNOW that I'm at his house. I should probably have guessed. Were they clues, the plate in the sink, the knife on the plate, the butter and jam smeared on the knife? Was it Francis's hair tangled in the comb in the bathroom? Did he still use a straight razor to shave, were his jeans still ripped at the knees?

Évelyne keeps the sewing kit in the laundry room cupboard. That I do see. I open the doors to the cupboards.

"It's just a formality, I hope that's okay," I explain to Évelyne, who is still nothing more to me than a woman my age, a bit younger or a bit older—at some point people become an indistinct mass, we feel the same age as women ten years younger or five years older and say, *Who cares anyway,* all the while thinking, *Now that's a lie if ever there was one.*

Évelyne gives a little laugh, sad and lingering. "Go ahead, open up all the cupboards, I have nothing to hide."

It's true. Her laundry room is spotless. Her sewing kit fascinates me, an elephant-grey crushed wool case embroidered in red cross-stitch, a gorgeous little Scandinavian novelty, and I think, *Évelyne is Danish.* She's a head taller than I am and her blond hair, straight and windswept as wheat, cascades down her black sweater.

I ask her.

She takes it as a compliment, of course, and says she's from Shawinigan.

I congratulate her on her house, which they'll have no trouble selling. She covers her eyes with her hand, and I know what's coming—I do this week in, week out. Guessing each client's household drama has become second nature to me, and on our most cynical of days, we place bets back at the office.

31 Des Groseilliers is a divorce. He cheated on her. She prefers the suburbs.

7678 Drolet always saw herself spending her golden retirement years in Sutton with the money she'd make from the sale, but her son pushed her to remortgage three times. She hadn't taken that eventuality into account.

10821 Turnbull was told that Ahuntsic is nowhere near as hot a market as Saint-Lambert.

Évelyne, at 794 Gouin East, woke up one morning to the man lying next to her blubbering. He told her he was suffocating, that he had to leave, he didn't know why, it wasn't her, but of course it was her, and anyway the children were older, old enough, eight is old enough, they'll be all right and anyhow there was nothing for it, he was suffocating he was dying he had to leave.

Usually, my colleagues and I laugh. Yet when Évelyne's eyes misted over, I held out a tissue and had no desire to tell the others afterwards.

"The place I'm moving to is smaller. An apartment. It's nice though. I don't think I could stand too much space."

"No, smaller's easier. Not as much housework."

Dimwit. She's not talking about housework and you know it.

"Do you think it will sell?"

Évelyne is crying in earnest now. I take her hand. I say yes, her house is fabulous. I myself would buy it if I could. It will make some other family happy, just as it did hers for so many years.

My client nods; I can tell she finds the idea comforting—all my clients do. There's some solace in thinking your house will live on outside you, like an extension of yourself, a promise renewed no matter the trials or failures, bestowing sudden meaning on sorrow. Personally, I have a hard time swallowing the whole idea because I have no desire to see others blossom where I wilted—but then I'm not that nice a person.

Évelyne shows me the rest of the house, starting with two children's bedrooms. In the first, a quilt in a delicate buttercup and peony pattern, cream-coloured, pink, pale green. A number of lively drawings on the walls, all signed SOLÈNE. In the other bedroom, blue and green stripes, dinosaur figurines, red-painted wood letters on the door: MATTÉO. Évelyne was astute enough to keep the walls white. It will be easier for visitors to project their own lives onto them—nothing worse than a pink bedroom covered in princess decals for undermining the morale of a mother with two sons who longs for the daughter she never had and hopes her new abode will offer the secret formula that will finally guarantee her the perfect family she's aspired to since childhood. To that client, I'll respond with all the solicitude I can muster, *Who knows, this house could be a lucky charm,* but when the client, in the throes of guilt at having diminished the worth of the children she does have, grabs hold of my arm, *My boys are wonderful, I love them so much, anyhow, what counts is that they're healthy, no? Do you have children?* and I reply, *Yes, three boys,* for the space of a second, she'll be caught between wanting to be me and relief that she's not. Her coral lips stretch into the saddest smile ever smiled and she'll murmur: *Three boys. Quite something, isn't it.*

I point out the lilac bush to Évelyne, the one we can see from the office window, say again that spring's a

good time to sell, that May's colours will be phenom-
enal here. She laps up my realtor-speak obediently and
with a slight lag time, as when you've had a bit too
much to drink the night before. Or when you've been
on a crying jag. By the window, her skin with its few
near-black beauty spots takes on an almost milky tint.
I find her painfully beautiful and think, *Her husband
must have been suffocating something fierce.* Who walks
out on a woman like her? I refrain from saying as much
to Évelyne — I don't want to see her tears flow again. I
promised the boys lasagna tonight, and there's no flour
left for the béchamel.

It's in the master bedroom that I find the most clues
pointing to a breakup. The wood is light in tone and
the sheets are white. One idea obsesses me: *She's Danish, and he walked out on her anyway.* Red felt slippers
are tucked neatly under the bed. Despite the order
Évelyne likes to keep in her home, there is something
concealed here, as in the sanitized crime scenes on TV
police procedurals, where a constellation of blood stains
is revealed under a black light. That's what their room
is like — bloody and impeccable.

Along with the pile of books on the bedside table, I
make out a magazine for do-it-yourselfers — it's a special issue on building sheds. Also a Bob Dylan biog-
raphy. Romain Gary's *Your Ticket Is No Longer Valid*. A
tidy pile. Later I'll remember this and think, *God, he*

hasn't changed a bit, even down to his enduring fascination with difficult, talented men.

On the other side of the bed, *Évelyne's side*, a glass of water, a charger, a number of open magazines, their pages wavy from bathtub reading, a small bottle of Tylenol, a Playmobil figurine and crumpled tissues.

Évelyne still sleeps here. Not him.

She sweeps away the tissues, the Tylenol, the Playmobil figurine, with an apology, "Please Évelyne, no need to apologize," and the sound of her name prompts Évelyne to collapse into my arms, sobbing. I can feel the Playmobil man's little hand dig into my shoulder. *The lasagna will have to do without the béchamel this time.*

"WHENEVER YOU THINK OF the future, you never picture this moment. You see carefree travel, wide-open car windows, a positive pregnancy test, treehouses, fights followed by sessions of making up, your lover adding years to his age without growing old. You see all that's pretty and smells good and gives you a rush and makes your blood run hot. You don't see...this."

Évelyne speaks softly but in a purposeful rush, as though convinced that the telling of secrets can only last so long; shame could silence her any minute now, and once again she'll have to shoulder her burden that grows heavier by the day, like a balled-up towel on the balcony that keeps absorbing rainwater.

With her back turned to me, she packs coffee into the filter, foams some milk, then stops, not turning around.

"I've made you coffee, but I'd rather have wine. How about you?"

The feverishness that comes in times of crisis. Permission to do the unexpected. I notice that, despite it all, I envy her.

"Bring on the wine!"

"You're sure?"

"I'm sure."

"Because I don't want to drink alone."

"I'll accept nothing less than a glass of wine and I refuse to drink alone."

Évelyne smiles and goes to pull an open bottle out of the fridge. She covers her left hand with her right, but too late—I can see it shaking. She had wine last night, nothing excessive, it helps, she doesn't like to take sleeping pills. She sits down and we sip from our glasses, comfort at hand. There's a crack in the plaster on the kitchen ceiling just above the door leading out to the backyard. Nothing to worry about. All the same, it should be looked after.

"When we first moved in, I wondered—will one of us die here someday?"

She apologizes for the morbid thought and half-laughs nervously. I should say, *Don't worry, I ask myself the same question every day. Will my life end here in this old car, its floor littered with candy wrappers and rotting apple cores? Will this ugly* IKEA *parking lot be my final destination?*

But Évelyne's tears well up, and I don't want to see

them fall again or have her ask questions to change the topic and then have to answer her. I may have thought that I envy her, but actually, I don't envy her at all.

"You're not morbid. Just the opposite. In real estate, we never talk enough about a house's potential for fatalities."

Évelyne looks surprised.

"That double gas range and its six burners are perfect for anyone bent on self-immolation."

She laughs, a fleeting melody. I'm on a roll.

"That cedar veranda is ideal for triggering heart attacks."

She dries her tears. "My ex'll like your sense of humour when he meets you."

"Does he like your sense of humour?"

"Way back when, yes, I suppose he did."

"I'm sorry, Évelyne...It's five thirty. My kids'll be ready to sic social services on me."

By now, Évelyne radiates a calm sadness. We belong to a club, the club of women who don't talk about love the way infant formula commercials do, and yet with each sentence, each fold of our exhausted eyelids, we speak of love and nothing else.

An hour later, I still don't know, after a bottle of white wine and an agreed-upon listing price and the posting of a for-sale sign, that it's his house I'm leaving. All I know so far is that he has walked out on her and that Évelyne's beauty didn't save her; she's in love and suffering. All so incredibly ordinary.

AT HOME, THEY'VE been waiting for me for a while. Oscar leaps into my arms and asks why I came home so awfully late. Boris shoves a complex Lego building into my face, recounting each and every stage that went into its creation. All I can hear of Philémon is his voice, a cavernous echo coming from the den where he and his freckles are busy soaking up the blue-tinged light of the computer screen. All three are here; they've survived their day in the city, the metro and school, the ham in their sandwiches, French dictation, smog, the mediocrity of their school. No one's throwing up or crying, and I can smell tomato sauce; Jim has started dinner. When he sees me walk into the kitchen, he gives me a kiss, tastes the wine on my lips, and laughs, "Got another client drunk, did you?" He tells me the parents' meeting at the school has been postponed, so we're free to indulge in an eveningful of episodes of the Welsh crime show we like so much. There's a magnetic pull to his shoulder; I rest my head. "It's like a dream come true," I say, and even though, deep in my heart rotting from easy living and death wishes, I know it's a bit of a lie—how else can I explain the dizziness, the jelly legs, the roiling innards, it could be the wine, but the dizziness the jelly the roiling were all there this morning, it's true this is a good life, a great life, like Évelyne's before it collapsed, a landslide, so I say no more, stop at *It's like a dream come true*, and Jim is happy, he taps my bottom, and now Oscar calls for me, and everything goes on as before.

THE BRIDGE JUST HAS to fit into the trunk of the car. It consists of a hundred or so Popsicle sticks assembled with white glue and built by Philémon and two of his sidekicks in sixth grade for their final science fair project. It is of the utmost importance that nothing fall on the bridge and that it be delivered to the school without incident. Which I will do in an hour's time, after a quick detour to the drugstore to find plastic bed pads because five-year-old Oscar hasn't managed to go a whole week yet without wetting his bed, a problem neither Jim nor I want to draw attention to for fear of triggering an incurable social neurosis in our son or inspiring him to delve too far into the subject, which might lead him to discover that most psychopaths were bedwetters as kids and make him think that he, too, is a psychopath, which would be unfortunate since the fact is he simply has the smallest bladder on the continent and the greatest of thirsts just before bedtime. I'll have to remember to hide the pads in a bag under the back seat. The other mothers from the science fair organizing committee mustn't see them. Otherwise, they'd feel they had free rein to remind me — without any prompting whatsoever on my part — that their children were potty trained by the age of two and that they hope Oscar doesn't have *a more serious problem?* I'd be forced either to smile with all my teeth (plus fillings) and tell a lie, *It's really only once in a while* (it isn't), or tear out their hair, its red highlights not fooling anyone, until they look like those forlorn dolls whose locks have been chopped off, their scalps full of holes like the ones in their brains. I may not be that nice a person, but I want to do well by my sons, so I don't forget to hide the mattress pads. I'll have to drop by Évelyne's as well for a set of her keys. People are already showing an interest and I'm delighted to think that a quick sale could go toward a new coat or a leather purse — that's the point of the job, making money. When Jim comes home from work, he often asks me what I've done today and I wonder what *done* means, and what *doing* meant at another time in my life, and the only thing that comes to my lips is, *I made money.* For the most part, it's an answer that satisfies me.

I don't know yet that I'm at his house, but it won't be long now, just a few more minutes as I step out of

the car, field a call on my cellphone. It's Jim, telling
me he'll be late tonight, he's playing badminton with
his friend Marco, and I imagine him — as every other
time he mentions badminton — racing across a waxed
wooden floor, his runners squeaking, dressed like a
private-school boy in an age-varied gang of similarly
dressed men. Why it is that I envisage them in gym
strips (burgundy shorts, grey T-shirts, vaguely medieval badges) I have no idea, but that's the way it is. I
hang up after confirming that I'll pick up our youngest and that, yes, the bridge is sitting in the trunk of
my car. I walk up the slate walkway ("superb modern
landscaping") to Évelyne's house, and the heel of my
shoe sinks into the wet earth between two slabs, of
course, I would have to traipse through mud. Not that
it makes much of a difference, with my hair scrunched
into an untidy bun and the elastic of my bra holding
by a thread. As I ring the doorbell, my only thoughts
are of faint contempt for myself and for the flowery
wrought iron doorbell, rustic and generic, *I'll have to
suggest Évelyne replace that, she must know the importance
of curb appeal, that doorbell is just tacky.* The explosive
contrast between the unfurling of my petty musings
and the bottomless, secular silence that descends on
me when the door opens is so marvelously tragic that
I can't even remember my own name.

"I THOUGHT SO. I thought it might be you."

"Because of the sign?"

"You could have included a picture. Then I'd have known for sure."

"No way. It's my last holdout against vanity."

"Says the girl in high heels."

"Mired-in-mud heels."

"Anyhow, I thought it might be you."

"But my last name's so common."

"There's no mistaking your first name."

"I've always said my first name is a ruse."

"Would you like a drink?"

"No, thanks. Why did you let her do it?"

"What?"

"Why did you let your wife hire an agent with my name?"

"Because I liked the idea."

"You liked the idea!"

"I didn't know it was you. But I like having your name in front of the house. It makes me happy."

"It 'makes you happy.'"

"Didn't the thought cross your mind?"

"No. I heard your name. I mean your first name. Évelyne brought it up several times, 'Francis built the bookcase, Francis knows more about the plumbing, Francis doesn't always answer my messages.'"

"But the thought didn't cross your mind?"

There is a sting to it every time. For years, even in a context that has nothing to do with him, with me, the name has still held its sting. Francis, the restaurant owner. Francis, my cousin's baby. Francis, Boris's friend in second grade. Francis Ford Coppola. A needle prick. Nothing more. Then life would go on as before. So no: "It never crossed my mind."

"And now here you are."

"And now, here I am. On the threshold of your house."

"The house I've put up for sale."

"The house your wife has put up for sale, yes."

"Évelyne's at a seminar in Toronto. She'll be back tomorrow."

"I'll call her."

"Are you going to tell her?"

"Tell her what?"

"Oh, sorry, I really think I should offer you something to drink."

"You did. I said no."

"We could have a seat."

"I don't think so."

"To talk. Just to talk."

"I don't think so."

"When was the last time?"

"I don't know, around the end of the century."

"You and your way with words."

"November 30, 1999."

"You do know then."

"I was waiting to see whether you did too."

"I don't remember the exact date, no."

"I'm not surprised."

"A real estate agent."

"That surprises you."

"Yes. I don't know, I imagined you in a university in Scotland teaching baroque vocals."

"Quite the imagination."

"But you saw yourself as a real estate agent."

"I didn't say that."

"So what then? What happened?"

"You've always been a tad stuck-up."

"That's true."

"A stuck-up engineer."

"An exhausted engineer right now."

"I came for the key."

"Right. The key."

"It'll wait till I can talk to Évelyne."

"Take the key."

"Mind you, I won't hide anything from her either."

"No?"

"No."

"Why not?"

"Because you don't break a woman who's already broken, especially not when you're broken yourself. It's an unwritten rule. *Solidarity among the ruins.*"

"We'll have to find another agent."

"Could be."

"How's business for you? Can you afford to lose a client?"

"No worries, bonehead. I'm thirty-seven. I've got three kids. Three. And lots of drooping skin."

"Oh well, I mostly drooped too."

"Ugh, how awful, what did I just say? I'm so sorry."

"No, it's me."

"God, Francis, what in the hell kind of conversation is this?"

"I know. One of our best."

"It's not funny."

"Sorry. I didn't mean it in a bad way."

"You never meant it in a bad way."

"You say that like it was some kind of problem."

"I've got to run. I have a bridge in my car."

THE THING ABOUT JIM'S hands is that they're miraculous. Large and padded like bear's paws, with bitten-down nails. Paddles. Early on, upon waking, I'd often find one of those big hands lodged under my hip where it had spent the night, a mooring of flesh. His hands surround me, engulf me, and in his hands, all moist space complies.

Jim is what could be called, when clichés don't turn you off, a man of few words. He slaves and strives and hammers away at life, his bear paws his only armour. The wild desire they inspire in me has never faltered.

His hands lay on my sweating brow when I was in labour. They stroke and knead my flat Irish ass. They lift Oscar up by his feet and carry him to the tub. His hands smell of wood and glue. In the orchestra, they glide back and forth on the trombone's slide, happy in their element. At ordinary times, his hands feed change into parking meters, spin the steering wheel, tie boot-laces. His hands have thrust me into a love bath and they keep me there, a welcome drowning.

Tonight, after I've brought my youngest home and done a load of laundry, I will hit social media to try to crush the pulsating memory of Francis's face. Then Jim will come home. I'm ready to give my life to feel his hand on the nape of my neck when he sidles up to me in the kitchen; I want it to leave its mark on me for the thousandth time and silence the churning that has been building in my blood for hours. But I won't be called on to give my life. Jim has never been stingy.

He comes home and his hands do my bidding, as on any other day. And yet. It seems to me that death from sorrow is a distinct possibility.

I'm in charge of goodies. Every year since Philémon turned six, I've prepared an assortment of sweets for the school's science fair. Last year, we sold six hundred items: cakes, cookies, Rice Krispie squares, small bags of caramel popcorn, and fudge. There's the organizing committee and its numerous meetings, the first one usually held on a dark windy Wednesday November evening during which no one has anything to say about an event to be held months later, but it's the main source of social interaction for some parents, so I go (one out of every three times) since I don't want to lose my kingdom. Philémon finishes elementary school this year, Boris will follow two years later, another six years down the road for Oscar. Then it'll be on to secondary school and they'll make a show of turning up their nose at my treats, especially in front of friends; their old mother will be relegated to her bedroom while her children are kept busy French kissing in the basement and speaking in a code only they are privy to, immersed in the mystery of youth and its hormones; in other words, one day, I will no longer be young again and I dread that moment, so I'm in charge of goodies for now, which gives me an inordinate amount of pleasure. I have singlehandedly whipped up six dozen homemade Oreo cookies. As I set up the sales table, I make crisp, straight lines with my cookies, Danh Ly's mother's macaroons on one side and Joséphine's mother's scones on the other. The pride I feel seeing my sons' friends pounce on the desserts I've prepared is as profound as it is ridiculous.

"I'm your shadow."

The girl is anything but a shadow: sixteen, taller than most boys her age, bright yellow jeans and a crocheted toque, she wears the forbidding expression of a comic book heroine. Next to her, my arms loaded down with boxes of apple juice, I look like a wet dog, and if you had to choose one of us as the other's shadow, there would be no contest.

"Excuse me?"

"My mother told me to come see you. I'm supposed to give you a hand. With the goodies."

She gives her name. *Simone.* Karine's daughter, yes — Karine offered to have her eldest give me a hand. Simone plunges her hands into the back pockets of her jeans and looks around with a certain preoccu-pied boredom. I assure her that I have often manned the goodies table on my own, and that she's free to leave if she wants to. But Simone shakes her head. I point at the small cash box; each item costs a dollar, and any whiner who thinks that's too expensive should be reminded that "The bake sale helps fund student activities like field trips and the purchase of comput-ers, and that if their heart is really that dark, they'd do better to eat a few cookies and lighten up." Simone gives a polite little laugh. We set to work, and nothing exists outside the taking of cash and the handing out of baking; it feels good to move, to forget, and Francis's grey, stormy, older face barely surfaces anymore. Fat and skinny, visiting grandparents and sweet-toothed teachers alike, they all hold out a hand and take, hold out a hand and take. Soon Simone slows down, trips up over the change, gets things wrong. "No, I told you a plain scone, not a fruit one!" Simone apologizes and adjusts her toque nervously. I turn to her, her cheeks are burning, "Are you okay?" She shakes her head as though to say *Don't talk about it, okay, just don't.* Then she says, so softly I have to lean in close to hear her, "I just saw someone." She searches him out again to see how far away he is, both afraid that she'll find him there and find him gone, and I say, "Take a break, go drink some water, Simone." She scurries off without giving Mehdi's family their change, so I look after it. I see her grab a friend by the sleeve and disappear into the gym washroom of this school that saw her grow up and where she probably fell in love with the boy she's just seen and has loved (in silence?) ever since. I think I spot him with his cocky smile and hopelessly banal fashion sense; then she returns a few minutes later, stony faced but determined and alive, and starts selling with renewed energy. To each her own end of the world.

He phones, not me. Some complicated number I've never seen before. *A poll.*

I've just closed the trunk, the plastic boxes that carried the haul of goodies piled up by the bridge, which Philémon insists on keeping as a souvenir. Next year, when his friends scatter to different high schools, they'll write every day to begin with, send each other videos, take open-armed selfies. Then one of them will stop responding to the chain of emails, another will announce he can't get together with the gang that weekend—he's meeting up with his new friends—and soon their orbits will shift, for better or worse, and childhood friendships will take on the delicate tint of a yellowing memento. Philémon, who unfortunately has inherited my propensity for nostalgia, still believes that the bridge from his last science fair will help cement his friendship with the other innocent, well-fed boys, and who am I to tell him otherwise?

In the back seat, Philémon and Boris are going through a play-by-play of the day's highlights (the explosion of Nicolas's beaker is in a near tie for first place with the escape of Léa's cat-cum-guinea pig). It's late, we are the last to leave the school. First, we had to count all the money, collapse the table, and pack everything up. Oscar wanted to stay, too, eager as he is to be in school like his brothers. But in the end, the sugar overdose did him in, and Jim took him home an hour before closing time. By now, he must be fast asleep, a few damp strands of hair clinging to his fighting spirit's brow. So the phone rings just as I close the trunk; if I dismiss the possibility it's a poll, the unknown number becomes more worrisome, *Jim's at the hospital with our youngest.* He did look kind of glassy eyed when he left. I had chalked it up to the sugar high, but maybe it's a case of encephalitis. How would we survive if we were to lose Oscar? And what about Philémon and Boris, living with the knowledge that they'd been spared, carrying the hideous burden of their own good luck?

"I'm sorry for calling so late."

Francis's voice is distant, and the line crackles as though the call were coming from James Bay.

"You have a funny number."

"What?"

"Your number. Your phone number."

"Oh. I'm calling from the office, that's why."

"Oh."

"I'm interrupting something."

"I've got a bridge in the car."

"Still?"

"The same one. It's come back."

Words are superfluous. Francis called. He is here, that's what counts. Words mean nothing, they don't fill the void, there is no void anyway, no air, nothing. Pure weightlessness. I lean back against the car. Philémon's eyes sweep over me, but he doesn't seem concerned. Thank God he can't see my expression, both relieved and confounded.

"I haven't had time to talk to your wife. It's been busy around here lately."

"No big deal."

"What about you? Did you talk to her?"

Clearly the question is whether he talked to her *about me*—for how many years have I wanted to hear him talk about me, no matter the reason? The wish seems so silly now that it's coming true. It all feels petty and pitiful—I'm thirty-seven now and have two sons sitting in the car, plus a third one asleep at home. (*He's not in the hospital! This call has nothing to do with him!*), damn it all to hell, am I not entitled to some semblance of dignity?

"No. I didn't tell her about you."

Francis didn't need any clarification; he's always been good at answering his own questions, *don't forget, don't forget, you idiot.*

"Listen, my boys are waiting."

"Oh. Sorry."

"Was there something in particular you wanted to say?"

"I wanted to..."

The wait. As you realize with terror and exultation that your expectations are as high as that very first day, a fever that never subsides, a candle stub consumed, the power has always and will always be in others' hands, and nothing, not time or children or bricks laid so fiercely, will dampen the dark desire to say yes to this man who's been gone for so long. *I wanted to* what?

"I wanted to see you. Not at my place. Just see you."

How long has it been since he left? Sixteen going on seventeen years? How many hours spent moaning that I longed to see him, *just see him*? Do we ever stop wanting what we desired so ardently at the age of twenty?

"Oh."

"I don't want to pressure you."

"No."

"Take your time."

"Yes."

"Friday, let's say at half past twelve, maybe out in front of Lenny's."

"Lenny's?"

"Remember?"

"Honestly."

"Okay then. Friday, half past twelve, in front of Lenny's."

"Francis."

"Yes."

"I might not show up."

"I know."

I have to hang up. I drop the phone into my pocket, pull out the keys to the car, open the door. I sit down and turn on the ignition. Stay alert to Philémon's and Boris's voices sharing stories of their day for the tenth time, asking if I've kept any Oreos for them. We drive past one of my listings and Boris says, "Yo, Mom, you're like a rock star agent now." I laugh, and it's not hard to laugh because Boris is funny and fabulous and Philémon is funny and fabulous. We pull up at the house, the boys carry the bridge inside without dropping it, and I send them off to make toast and honey before bedtime, with the usual instructions, "teeth, dirty clothes in the hamper, lights out in ten minutes." I act normal around Jim, kiss his forehead and complain about the parents on the committee. We watch the ten o'clock news. Then, blaming the smell of sugar and grease, I slip away to jump into the shower, locking the door behind me. The uproar of water pounding against the porcelain tub seems like permission, my heart now free to race off the charts, my hands to shake, as I murmur over and over, an obstinate ringing, *FridayFridayFriday.*

I have to remind myself that I'm thirty-seven years old with three children, and that all of this is ludicrous.

1982

IN MY EYES AND for the longest time, my mother shone. Not like a princess, nothing diamond studded or golden about her — Paule was all assymetrical strands of hair and skinny men's old T-shirts. Her shine emanated from her cavalier attitude, delinquency dressed in boys' clothes. She was Joan Jett but listened to Handel.

At thirty-two, my mother left Abitibi behind with her two children in tow. She formed a feral attachment to the city. Paule had always had and would always have black spruce where her bones should be. No, what she left behind was my father and a ten-year marriage, his spineless cruelty, the accumulation of broken promises — the narrow-mindedness of the place, *scandalous*, she would often say afterwards, the small-mindedness so paradoxical compared to the vastness of the Abitibi sky. She would be separated from my father for nearly twenty years before filing for divorce. She would never live in Abitibi again.

In Montreal, she felt surrounded by her own people. I would often grab for a stranger's leg in public places, wrap my arms tight, only to realize that the paint-spattered pants, the workman's boots, and perfume with its whiff of Craven A and sandalwood did not belong to my mother. Another woman in the city exuded the same mystery, the same beauty, despite her fingers strangled by too-heavy grocery bags, weighed down by the fatigue of those who don't have time to hope for more. When we arrived in 1982, Montreal was full of other my-mothers.

MORNINGS, SHE HURRIED AS we walked to daycare, her pace brisk, already annoyed.

"Get a move on, Tessa. Quit stopping to look at everything along the way."

Farther on, she'd slow down then stop. My hand clutched the branch, string, rock, candy wrapper I'd just picked up from the sidewalk a bit tighter, and I waited to see what was coming. "We're going to be late, we're already late, if I'm late to work, do you know what'll happen? I could lose my job and then who'd pay for groceries, the rent, the boots on your feet?"

I wanted to say, *Daddy's got money*. But her already sombre gaze would have darkened further. I thought, *She hates my father.*

I hadn't yet understood that no, what stretched her to the breaking point was the sustained effort she put into not disappointing me, not revealing my father's financial inconstancy; what set her lip to trembling was love. *I'm only thirty-two not old at all how did I turn into a harpy who yells and tells her daughter to quit stopping to look at everything she sees when that's exactly what she should be doing at the age of four at any age, how is that?*

So, more often than not, I held my tongue, dropped the branch the string the rock the wrapper, watched them fall and asked myself whether it hurt when they hit the ground.

ONLY FLEETING MEMORIES REMAINED of Abitibi, damp images that vanished quickly. My father's car, its leather seat burning my thighs after swimming at the lake; I had to sit on my wet towel not to get burnt, and I'd always forget. The smell of coconut lotion to soothe my raw skin felt uniquely comforting afterwards. The burn was a reminder of all the hours spent splashing in the crystalline waters of La Ferme Lake, shaking sand off our bathing suits, wolfing down hot dogs, searching for wild raspberries in the underbrush where hidden couples made out. Once I caught a glimpse of a woman's breast, then a man's sex. The wet friction of their flesh, the confusion of skin, the hairs, the thrusting, and the man's final groan would come to me at night, lying in bed, my body awake to the pulsing call of a Morse code I would only recognize much later as desire.

During trips to visit our great-grandmother who

smelled like eucalyptus and who my mother adored, we always stopped in at the Sullivan creamery where my orange ice cream cone would end up smeared in my hair and make me feel sick. Paule stood outside leaning against the car door, a slender silhouette with a cigarette in her hand, as we licked away the drops running down our thumbs, our palms, our wrists. Some always fell onto our thighs, mine plump and pale (*Two bleached ham hocks!* my paternal grandmother would cry whenever she saw them, and even though I didn't understand, it was clear that her words were no compliment), quickly mopped up with the hem of my T-shirt, no harm done. My mother was disheartened by the way I always tended to end up covered in sugar in all its forms. *Good God, what did I ever do to deserve such a slob for a daughter!*

Paule didn't believe in a god, even less so in his goodness. If I could just remember to wipe my mouth after dipping my slice of bread in maple syrup when no one was looking, erase any trace of melted chocolate from my fingers, throw away the Cellophane from the Kraft caramels I pilfered from my brother's Hallowe'en basket. If she didn't see me eating and no longer saw her daughter as a dirty little pig, then Tessa-the-slob wouldn't exist anymore, right?

ONE NIGHT, SHE TOOK us to her friends' place. She must have stopped seeing them soon afterwards, since, of their huge house chock full of books, Turkish carpets, and posters for exhibits held in faraway museums, all I remember is that one summer party when they brought all their tables out into the lush backyard (was it in Notre-Dame-de-Grâce somewhere? Or maybe Ahuntsic?) to make one long table covered in newspaper since we'd all soon be elbow deep in lobster claws and melted butter. Two hot plates had been set up on the grey veranda, its paint peeling off in spots, with huge aluminum pots to welcome the wriggling lobsters amid the joyous cries of older boys who intimidated me as much as they fascinated me. My brother wore a polite smile, his mouth a thin line to conceal his distress at the killing of those poor creatures. Later, he would eat with as much gusto as everyone else, but I knew the passage from the world of the living to the world of the dead bothered him, whether it be of an insect, a barbecue chicken, or a Christmas tree. Weren't they all sad to lose their lives?

After supper, the adults lingered around the table, full of wine and stories told a hundred times before.

"She had no panties on! She showed up for her thesis supervisor in a mini-skirt and pantyless!"

"Big deal, no one but me knew! I wanted to feel the power of my feminine mystique!"

"Hon, you've got Betty Friedan all wrong!"

"I definitely get her better than you, dude..."

"Hey, Marc, did you know Suzanne defended her thesis commando?"

And off they went again. Paule laughed like everyone else. Pretty well every time I walked by on my search for dandelions with the hosts' daughter (what was her name again, she had such a pretty wildflower wallpapered room and a white wicker desk, straight out of my dreams), my mother grabbed my arm and pulled me to her to shower me with kisses, one of her rare displays of affection that I took stiffly then missed as soon as they were over. Inside, the boys had spread comic strip albums out on the floor and were lost in stories of pirates and of Gauls.

The white-wicker girl led me to her parents' bedroom, which had the biggest bed I'd ever seen. "It's a king," she pronounced like someone in the know. I nodded without a word, *Be careful not to show how ignorant you are.* Then she pulled a pile of books from under the bed and laid them out on the quilt with a feverish look. She began turning the pages of a comic book that must have been for adults only, you could tell right away by the images of big-busted women and men swigging beer straight from the bottle. The girl placed a plump finger *(What a pretty ring with its sapphire stone! What if I took it from her while she slept?)* on one of the pictures. A giant, naked woman lay stretched out on the prairie. She was asleep, her mouth partially open. She took up the space of several houses and the church steeple only reached her ear. Her legs were spread and her sex was hairy. It was then that I noticed a little man climbing inside her with the help of another elf pushing him in headfirst. Elves clung from her breasts; others tried to clamber up her thigh. Looking at her face again, I saw she wasn't asleep. Instead she was smiling, eyebrows raised, with the same focus I'd glimpsed on the lovers in the underbrush at the lake. "They're doing sex," I said, and the girl added, "Uh-huh, they're doing sex and, at the end, the elf pees in her mouth." We didn't speak. There was still so much we had to learn about the mystery behind why this image was both exciting and repulsive. Even the girl with the princess room knew that.

I WONDERED WHY MY mother's friends had such pretty houses while we lived in a two-bedroom apartment on Saint-Viateur above a store that sold handbags. Weren't they all alike, these grown-ups who drank Black Label beer at five, then wine with their guinea fowl à la Meaux mustard? Didn't they all have the same Léo Ferré LP and the same *"oui"* badges hidden under the socks in their underwear drawers to forget the tears they'd shed over the May 1980 referendum? Didn't they all speak out against politicians' shocking bills? My mother's friends were university professors, social workers, civil servants — there were a few eccentrics thrown into the mix: the guy who grew garlic whose black beard was so thick his nose was barely visible, the woman who sold second-hand Indonesian furniture in a tiny boutique on Saint-Denis, but the others seemed to lead tranquil lives in their houses still sporting "original stained glass" and their fridges always crammed full of individual yogurt containers. At home, we bought puffed rice cereal in bulk and stored it in glass jars that we kept in plain sight atop the kitchen water heater next to the gas furnace.

Paule left every morning to work as a secretary for a sweaty, red-faced man with tight curly hair who ran an import–export business. She hated her job. When I'd lie at her feet on the living room floor, drawing pictures (mermaids first, and singers later), I'd sometimes overhear her on the phone: "I can't quit, we're in the middle of a recession. Things are only supposed to get worse. There'll never be any benefits or security. At least I've got a paycheque." Her friends spoke of collective bargaining, angry unions, hard-fought-for benefits not to be lost at any cost. My mother kept quiet, poured herself a drink and nodded, gazing out the window, cut off from the world, staring at the powerlines in the distance or at a fall maple tree turning red. At those times, she couldn't have been more different than her friends and she couldn't have been more alone.

YET THERE WERE OTHER delicious days when she was
fully present and accounted for. It was immediately apparent. She'd have a skip to her step when she came
home from work. She'd bring bags full of fruit and puff
pastry and would sometimes have had enough time
to stop in at the bookstore and buy the new American
novel she'd heard about on the radio. On those days,
Paule loved to talk. She talked about her day at the office, memories from her childhood spent counting her
grandmother's buttons and bobbins, her birth stories,
spectacular and funny. We loved to listen. With supper
done, we'd ask her to walk with us over to the park or
down Laurier to window-shop after the stores were
closed, and she'd agree. On the way there, she'd never
tell us to hurry up and would stop with me in front
of the flowery skorts at Deslongchamps that I coveted
with near-troubling ferocity. "We'll make our own,

clothes to fit our own taste, it won't cost as much," she'd say, trying to convince me. She promised that on our next trip to our grandmother's, we'd borrow her sewing machine. Then we loitered on the steps to the church for a good while, long enough for me to walk their entire length, imagining myself on a tightrope above a river full of crocodiles. When she announced, "Time to go home," her voice had nothing of its usual bored, fatigued tone. This time around, going home held the promise of bubble baths, stories read from cover to cover, and hot milk before bedtime.

The next morning, her eyelids would be heavy once more, and when she growled at Étienne to get out of the bathroom, I knew that the break in the clouds had closed. Still, I looked forward to the next interlude the way you look forward to a letter, or to spring.

AT NAPTIME, WE HAD to lie down on royal blue gym mats held together with worn Velcro. The daycare, both a refuge and a lion's den, was steeped in cooking smells: Chinese-style macaroni, vegetable soup, cabbage rolls. Hot, salty food, mouthfuls of onions and soya sauce. At home, we didn't eat the same kind of meals; Paule was determined to have us eat like adults — or was it simply that she didn't want to stoop to the level of "family fare"? When she brought a rack of lamb to the table, maybe it didn't remind her that she was a single mom as much as a meatloaf would have. In any case, food at the daycare was attuned to the times and I had no complaints. When naptime rolled around, all that was left of lunch were the lingering smells and reassuring clink of thick pink plastic dishes being washed in the kitchen. They put on soft music for us that I recognized and replayed non-stop in my head, unable to sleep. Lying on the plasticized mattress cover, a tiny blanket (never heavy enough, never warm enough for me to fall asleep) over my shoulders, I spent the allotted hour fastening and unfastening the Velcro on the mat. Keeping jerky time to the lullabies. I'd be warned, then stop. And start up again. What else was there to do? How else could I spend eternity until I gained access to the grown-up world? I examined the posters on the wall—hand hygiene, required winter clothing, how to settle disputes between friends. Blond birdlike girls and freckle-cheeked boys. I always looked more like the boys than the girls in the posters because of my snarled hair and sticky fingers. I stared at the exercise ladders, counted the number of rungs to the top then back down again, reciting the alphabet. At the bottom of the ladder, I'd only made it to "P" and so had to go up again to end with "Z." Letters, numbers, the harp in the lullabies, the Velcro, the blue, the sleeping faces. (How did they do it? How were they lucky enough to gain access to oblivion?) Their limp bodies were an irresistible draw, and sometimes I'd run my fingers over one child's knee or another's wrist, just to measure how asleep they were. I didn't want to wake them. Maybe by touching them, I'd have access to their world. Sometimes I would place my pinkie on a playmate and leave it there for minutes at a time, until my fingers started to tingle. I soon found the fixed position as unbearable as when my mother, ignoring the fuss I'd make and the fact I was forever losing them, forced me to wear those small fitted leather gloves. Only then would I pull my hand away and roll over on my island of a mat to stare at the large round clock above the window, its big hand on six, another half-hour to go, but I had run out of numbers and letters and tired my finger out on Claudia's knee or Bobby's wrist. The lullabies had died down; the only sound remaining was that of the regular breathing in and out. *Patience, Tessa. Patience.*

The Bathing Suit

First-time buyers can be spotted from miles away. Their bodies are taut with excitement. They're literally poised on the threshold of everything to come. For them, the process takes on a symbolic hue: the handing over of keys, the pen they use to sign the purchase offer, the weather on the day they visited the house. Tanya and Marc are no exception to the rule. A few days ago, I showed them a condo by the Lachine Canal, and it was love at first sight.

I'm the listing agent for Steve, a banker now determined to make his fortune in Toronto. He was rarely home. On top of working twelve-hour days, Steve would spend the rest of his waking hours at the gym or in restaurants frequented by Canadiens players, and saw no reason to decorate the condo's interior. "That's girlie stuff," he told me with a wink. I took it as a generous gesture: he was under no obligation to wink at his real estate agent, especially given that I'm at least twelve years older than he is and that, in his eyes, I must have about as much sex appeal as a Christmas tree. Tanya and Marc found neither the sad ecru walls or the laminated pictures that Steve clearly inherited from the show condo when he moved in depressing. Tanya labelled the look *interesting*, adding, "The pictures bring out the mahogany in the kitchen cupboards." I said, "You should consider a career in real estate." Her face shut down. "Maybe after the treatment's done." Marc shot me a look of dismay, a look that proclaimed, *Change the subject, let's not go there, my life is nothing but one extended discussion of Tanya's goddamn fertility treatments.* But before I could lead them over to the walk-in closet, Tanya had aired the whole story: six years of trying, including two with the help of drugs, only to realize that in vitro fertilization was their only hope, the side effects of the hormones were tough, Marc was so patient, and she still had hope. When I said *three boys* in answer to the usual question ("Do you have any children?"), her face registered a multitude of expressions: surprise, admiration, sorrow, envy. "Three boys! How wonderful! That's really wonderful! Did you hear that, Marc? Three little boys."

Right then and there, I decided that I liked Tanya and that I would to the bitter end, even if she had a thing for mahogany cupboards and contemplated putting a waterbed in their bedroom.

Today, Tanya shows up for our meeting in an overpriced café on Viger carrying a jar of jam. "For our guardian angel," she says, handing it to me. "It's my raspberry jam. I pick the raspberries myself with my mother every summer on my parents' farm in Saint-Hyacinthe. Children usually like raspberry jam, don't they? Do yours?"

I thank her — "Yes, they love it" — and am surprised as I slip the jar into my purse to feel a tightness in my throat and my eyes blinded by tears. This young woman bursting with simple, profound needs moves me and reflects my own darkness back at me. Marc chimes in, tells me how it was Tanya's jam that seduced him, says, "Feed a man, and he's yours for life." Usually, I'd delight in the cliché's pathetic lack of originality, but Marc places his hand on Tanya's and Tanya's fingers squeeze his. The two are alone, together in their suffering, and everything in them is magnified, so I put a sock in it. They are love, and the only thing left for me to do is to just shut the hell up.

"Do you think five thousand below the asking price is a reasonable offer?"

Marc has gone all earnest on me. His hair, normally hidden under a New York Yankees ballcap, is slicked back today like a real gentleman's; of the typical suburban dweller, the kind you see in spades at sports bars, almost nothing remains. Broad shouldered as he is, Marc looks like yet another fine, upstanding citizen. But he's worried. Tanya hasn't liked a single condo other than this one. For the past few months, he's had to give her a daily shot in the thigh; they've made the same trip, sometimes three times a week, to the fertility clinic on Décarie to check the number of follicles she produces, most often returning home no further along, *We'll see in two days' time.* They've waited for calls that never came. Tanya stumbled on a diet that a group of women on the Internet swore by. Marc added the address for a Vietnamese herbalist who worked miracles for a colleague's wife to his smartphone. Tanya has preceded and followed every medical procedure with an acupuncture session; it worked for Céline Dion, "Just look, she has three boys now too." Marc has masturbated in the clinic's pistachio-green windowless room trying not to think of his child since that would be *wrong*, but how could he not, because what else was he doing there if not making a child?

Nothing was spoken, but in the nervous hand with which he stroked his nascent beard over and over, in his fear of losing a condo for want of five thousand dollars, Marc came across loud and clear: *Tanya and I need some good news.*

"I think it's a very reasonable offer. Honestly, you could even bring the price down a bit more."

Tanya shakes her head. "No, I don't want to lose it."

"The market's slow, and the condo's been up for sale since last fall."

"Yes, but there are other showings planned."

"That's true, but the only other offer was lower than yours. And it was accepted."

"Why didn't it work out?"

"The buyer backed out. He couldn't get his financing."

Tanya studies Marc's face, looking for peace of mind. "I don't know. I really want this to work."

"Even if you offer ten thousand less than the asking price, I'm pretty sure they'll accept."

"Pretty sure, but not positive."

"Right."

"We could take that sun vacation, babe."

Marc wants to believe; his eyes on me are those of a boy asking his dad if roller coasters really are safe. But Tanya is terrified; another disappointment and, worse, one she could have avoided, would do her in.

"Okay, we'll stick to five thousand. We just won't go as far for our holiday."

"The condo'll be a holiday! It's got an indoor pool!"

Tanya takes a deep breath (*How unfair, really, with her toned body and camp counsellor tan, that she's having such trouble conceiving when pale, old, flabby-skinned me got pregnant in no time at all, who can believe there's some intelligent plan out there in the face of such an obvious screw-up?),* her face lights up, and she quickly signs. "This is what we need, love. I can feel it."

I'm CURSING MYSELF. I have to admit that I didn't pick either the best time or place, but it is what it is. It was my great idea to wait till now to buy myself a swimsuit, scarcely two hours before my first mommy-and-me swimming lesson with Oscar. *No big deal, just a minor detail*, I kept telling myself to avoid the issue, *five minutes and I'll be done*. But I've been wandering like a ghost through the aisles of Sports Experts in Rockland Centre for over forty minutes wearing a pathetic expression at the sorry displays of one-piece bathing suits offered up for my consideration. For anyone the least bit concerned with modesty (by modesty, I mean *simple courtesy*), the selection is depressingly austere. Suits with wide reinforced straps and flesh-coloured lining. Suits with unforgiving necklines that hearken back to another time. Hibiscus and pineapple patterns as wretched as rain. Obviously, I hadn't expected any given suit to call out to me — I haven't expected as much for a very long time — but the offering is so catastrophic, so demoralizing, that I think I just might collapse right here and now, stretched out between the racks on Sports Experts' geometrically patterned carpet and wait to die. Instead, I make a supreme effort and turn to the selection of two-piece swimsuits — whether out of sheer bravado or madness, it's hard to say.

That's when I catch sight of her. She has a few years on me as is apparent by the care she's taken with her makeup; she's past the stage where a woman can leave the house with no makeup on. She's standing in front of the bikini section, a cute striped bikini bottom between her fingers, imagining wearing it in public. A wicked flash of glee in her eye is immediately followed by a small tic as she hastily returns the bottom to the hanger before a salesclerk can suggest she take it to a change-room. Then she sees me watching. In that fraction of a second, her shame and mine conjoin; we are one and the same, and I curse her as much as I curse myself for exposing myself once again. What should we have done to avoid the ordeal? Where should it have started? Should I have had a beauty queen for a mother, sacrificing her weekends to drag me from ballet class to aerobics so that, from my youngest years, I would learn that my body was a temple to swimsuits? Should she have snatched her daughter's beloved books from her hands, all the better to send her off swimming, diving, running, skipping until she developed an athlete's firm, discreet breasts? Had we not been attentive enough, had we no conception of everything that needed doing to ensure that today, under Sports Experts' neon lights and the syrupy, pitying gaze of saleswomen who, themselves, *knew what needed to be done*, we could take hold of the teensy two-piece suit without shame or fear?

In a rush, the stranger chooses a brown suit with gold trim. Like me, she has understood that to be coquettish a swimsuit must forego severity, and that, by and large, an aging bourgeois version is preferable to a priggish version. I nod imperceptibly at her choice, giving silent assent, and feel she does the same when she sees my choice of a black rather sporty suit whose crossed straps manage to hint at a semblance of joie de vivre. But there'll be no revelatory moment. The great reconciliation between women and their bodies will not take place here, in the heart of Rockland Centre.

AT THE POOL, THE contact between our cold feet and the ceramic tile doesn't take our mind off the looming need to get undressed. Wearing our coats, our spring boots, our earrings, and, for a few of us, our tailored suits bestowing a semblance of importance, a desire for elegance, in no time we find ourselves confined to badly locked stalls where we wriggle into our bathing suits, relics of our disappointment, while trying not to let our clothes get wet on the floor. At the same time, we must keep our children from opening the door to the stall before we're ready since the one thing worse than having to wriggle into a swimsuit one April evening is doing so in full view. Elastics snapping on thighs. Straps digging into flesh. Repositioning, levelling of breasts, creating symmetry. Oscar has been ready for ages and waits for me in his plaid swimsuit, too tight since last winter. The rubber strap to his goggles is

twisted; patiently he straightens it out. His small belly
with its folds, as pale as mine, that expands and empties
to the rhythm of his little boy breath—my heart breaks
for the thousandth time at his beauty and nonchalance.
His total lack of self-consciousness shatters me; how I
regret my self-condemnation. How much time have I
wasted railing against this body that created Oscar's? In
a sudden desire for redemption, I long to loll in serenity,
take stock of my strengths and all the wonder in my
life, reflect on it, why not start a blog, be done with the
devil, pulverize him with kindness!

I step out of the stall and run into Ève, who greets
me as she drags her twins to the pool, her white bikini
snug against the tanned washboard of her abdomen and
her shock of hair that can only be described as sexually
active; yes, she's insufferable. I pull at the elastic to my
suit to be sure half a buttock isn't hanging out, my body
and its constellation of winter rashes reminding me that
kindness has never erased a single stretchmark. *Moron.*
How could you have thought for one second that, in less than
forty-eight hours from now, you would be able to take your
clothes off in front of Francis? Because that's what this is all
about, isn't it? When you try on a swimsuit in a store that
you then buy, when you look at yourself in a mirror on the
way into the pool, then at your reflection in the glass in the
lifeguards' office, and then in the window's reflection, it's
him you're thinking of. You imagine him scrutinizing the

body he once knew, a body now altered, wilted, a body that was far from a rose to begin with, a cheap daisy at best or that purple flower that grows along the ditches in Amos, the kind we chewed on for its sweetness—a useful flower, what was its name, it doesn't matter, you get my drift. Is that what this is, moron? Yes, it is, this horrible, crass desire to commit adultery as you hold the flutter board for your son and he paddles his feet in the water.

JIM'S AWAY AT A concert. Whenever he's gone, the boys never ask where he is. He often travels, it's true; his profession involves some forty concerts every year, not counting all the tours and festivals. It's all written down on the scout calendar. All three know their dad's routine: he shows up at 6:30 p.m. at the concert hall carrying his trombone in one hand and his pressed tuxedo in the other. He greets his colleagues, Gerry the percussionist, Bernard the bassoonist, and Sophia the violist. They joke around to calm their nerves, and then Jim warms up among his fellow musicians in the cacophony typical of any orchestra tuning up. At 7:15, he changes, ties his bowtie, laces his shoes, smooths back his hair. At 7:45 or so, he calls us. He rarely talks about the orchestra's programme. Jim has no need for compliments. He calls and asks whether Boris's oral presentation is ready, "Is Oscar's teacher still on sick leave, did Philémon eat his lunch?" He wants to know how I'm doing. How it went at the pool today. I choose not to mention my excursion to Sports Experts. As with yesterday and the day before that, I choose not to say a word about Francis. I'm not accustomed to lying to Jim. But before this, there was no reason to lie. I pour the contents of a package of linguine into boiling water (pasta for the third time this week) and the cloud of steam serves to dissipate, somewhat, the cloud of my guilt.

"Nervous?"

"No, I'm okay. By now, we could play with our eyes closed."

"Me, too, I know the evening's program off by heart. That doesn't stop me from freaking out."

Jim's sigh. Not in irritation, just empathy. The man loves me.

"The boys acting up?"

How can I tell him the boys have nothing to do with it? That the only person acting up here is me?

"No, I'm just joking. Everything's fine."

A few months ago, in a downtown boutique, the kind of place that camouflages the mediocrity of its merchandise behind a "rustic" decor, I found a distressed T-shirt inscribed with the words, *Everything's fine.* The irony, intentional or not, amused me. I bought it and often wear it. As for Jim, my hard edge amuses him, invigorates him, attracts him. He maintains the T-shirt is free of irony. Everything really is fine. He often says, *Everything's going so much better than I could have imagined.*

"I love you, you know. Sit them down in front of the TV if things get worse."

"Been there, done that, captain."

"See you later, honey."

The water rises, boils over, spreads starch over the glass-ceramic stovetop burners, which begin to smoke. I curse and hurry to pour the contents into a colander in the sink. Another blast of steam, another sigh leading me to squeeze my eyes shut. Is this when everything changes? Is this when my story falls apart?

As I was saying, the boys don't really notice when Jim's away. What if I were the one who didn't come home? At first, my disappearances would be fleeting; generally speaking, I'd be here except for one or two nights a week. Would they notice? At first, probably. Oscar would wander through the house, call my name, not understand. But he'd get used to it. It's possible to get used to anything. One evening, two, five, a whole week.

A whole month.

Everyone would get used to it. Therein lies the tragedy.

AFTER EIGHT, THE HOUSE's rhythm changes. Only
Philémon stays up till nine o'clock, and the silent lull—
both of us careful not to rouse Boris and Oscar—re-
minds me of another time. The two of us, Philémon and
I, alone. Born as Jim was finishing his studies, Philémon
quickly became our third roommate. I took him everywhere, determined not to let myself be cut off from the
world, and we'd sit, he in his stroller, me on benches
in parks I visited on a rotating basis—Laurier, Jarry,
Jeanne-Mance, Maisonneuve, Westmount, La Fontaine.
We watched the seasons unfold. Philémon was a serious, attentive baby, extremely diligent in the business
of living. He slept, drank, watched, and cried with the
same painstaking attention, as though fulfilling an ar-
duous task. The force of my unrelenting love for him
during those first months both revived and terrified me.
Now, on evenings when Jim is at work, Philémon sits

in the living room wearing his big red headphones and playing his favourite songs. From time to time, he taps on the touch screen, texts with friends, maybe a girl or two. I leave him to his secrets. Because, despite the headphones and the dizzying speed with which he has grown since the day he was born, he is still the same, beside me on the couch, and although I start reading an article on Obama's second term and Philémon listens to his music, we're just as before. Watching the seasons unfold together.

I WAKE WITH A start when Jim comes home just before midnight. The familiar sound of the key in the door, his trombone being set down on the floor, and the flush of the toilet, everything I normally find so reassuring now instills panic, nausea, and I turn on the bedside lamp. Have I forgotten anything? I know I remembered to erase the search history on my laptop after an hour spent trying to track down first Francis then Évelyne and their children. I wanted to see pictures of him. Articles on her. Have their — adorable — children done any commercials? Been part of charming documentaries on Montreal, the PTA, or their school's Christmas traditions? Is their family famous for something, are they keeping an exceptional past a secret, did they ever make the news? I didn't come up with much. Évelyne trained as a psychologist, contributed articles to several research papers on pediatric mental

health, and teaches a course on psychoeducation at the
Université de Montréal. Her course this year is entitled
Assessing Developmental Delays. In 2013, a women's
magazine interviewed her in her expert capacity for an
article on disciplining autistic children. "You mustn't
forget that autistic children experience emotions too
but have difficulty expressing them in the way we do.
You must be particularly mindful of what their tan-
trums are telling you." Reading her words, I saw her
again, her tears streaming and her hand working at
the corkscrew. Évelyne, helpless, lost—worse yet, that
image had no trouble superimposing itself onto the
image of Évelyne the expert, shining hair, firm hand-
shake. I found nothing on him, other than his name in
a group picture: "Once again, RBQ's team of engineers
wins this year's golf tournament, congratulations!"
followed by the word *absent* in brackets. He has no
online presence; it's as though he's still living back in
1998, just as I've been picturing him all these years.
My search left me frustrated and distressed. *Évelyne's
suffering,* I keep telling myself. *Évelyne will suffer from
all this.* The realization hits me as Jim walks down the
hall to our bedroom and to me, my face bathed in the
glow of the laptop, checking for the third time that
I've erased all traces.

He opens the door quietly, thinking I'm asleep, not
wanting to disturb me since he knows what a light

sleeper I am. Jim's happy to see my eyes are open, not that he'd say as much, but I know he likes me to be awake when he comes home. He sits down next to me, one hand on my cheek, the other in my hair, his lips on my eyes, my nose. Jim's infinite tenderness erases almost everything else. Concerts and hockey games charge him up, make him want me. Or maybe he chooses to relinquish that energy, to hand it over to me. Whether it's desire he feels or the desire to desire me makes little difference; it's still a prodigiously generous choice that makes him, quite simply, irresistible.

I'm undressed in no time; he pulls off my panties without hesitation and it's natural for me to open my thighs and invite him in. The power of his instrumentalist's breath blocks out all other sounds, the boys could wake and come running and I wouldn't hear them, there is nothing here but the wave we become, our breath, nothing but the concentrate we are, fifteen years of repeated, adored, necessary and mastered gestures, nothing else exists, he knows how to bring me back to life and make it possible for me to leave myself behind, these minutes are the gold of our existence to which I succumb, it feels so good so why are tears running onto the pillow, *why these tears that you blot away with the sheet, moaning your pleasure even more, if not because this, too, is propelling you to Friday, to that other man, the one you have yet to finish with, and Jim will suffer.*

The one sentence playing over and over in my mind, devastating, inadmissible, inevitable, *Jim will suffer, and I'm going to do it anyway.*

1993

We were fourth in line. Ahead of us, an older Anglo couple, a ballcap-wearing scalper, and a group of boys from Notre-Dame. I wanted to turn and head back to where I'd come from. The two of us, Sophie and I, stood there on Sainte-Catherine Street and our parents had no idea where we were, each of us having sworn we were sleeping over at the other's house, so if something bad happened to us (What? Weren't private-school boys the most twisted of all? I'd just finished reading *The Secret History,* I knew all about it), no one would ever know. Or at least not for a very long time, not before we'd been dumped, butchered breasts and all, into the river, but Sophie said, "Stop." She knew one of the boys, had met him at a Hallowe'en dance, and he was harmless. She sat on the sidewalk behind them and bummed a cigarette. I stayed standing. I had brought a sleeping bag and pillow, my backpack was chock full of provisions—nuts, two apples, a few 3 Musketeers bars, two Cokes—and I'd just figured out that I was the only one who brought anything. Summer was around the corner; we had only a few exams left before the holidays and the night air was mild. No one would need a jacket or a sleeping bag to keep warm. One of the private-school boys (he'd soon tell us his name was Olivier) handed around some gin; Sophie was already drinking from the metal canteen (one long swig), then it was my turn (an awkward fake sip). Naively, I had thought we'd be able to sleep. Wasn't that the plan? "Tess, let's sleep on the street to get tickets to Pearl Jam!" Sophie was determined we would be at the Verdun Auditorium come August and claimed there was no surer way than to sleep out front of the Spectrum; we would be the first at the box office as soon as it opened at ten. I offered to try phoning—I was ready to dial the same number a hundred times if necessary, and I was an early riser, really, it didn't bother me. But Sophie had insisted, and Étienne agreed. My brother wouldn't go to the trouble himself, not for Pearl Jam, too pop, but he assured me that if I really wanted to see Eddie Vedder in person, Sophie's approach was the way to go. Raph would be at the show too. In the cafeteria the day before, he'd told me his dad—a journalist—would have a press pass and take him along. As he spoke, he tucked a strand of hair far too blond to be reasonable behind his ear, making me feel as if I might very well drop dead or rip off all my clothes, and I decided then and there that nothing, not even my own cowardice, would stop me from finding a way to be there with him in August in the Verdun Auditorium.

So I'd brought my pillow and purple and green sleeping bag, ridiculous under the Spectrum lights, filled my backpack, knotted my plaid shirt around my waist, pulled on my army surplus boots, and followed Sophie. It was a quarter past midnight when Olivier offered us our first sip of gin, half past midnight when I managed to lay my pillow and sleeping bag on the ground behind Sophie, and 12:40 when Nico, Olivier's friend, asked for my name.

"Tessa."

"Tessa? Are you Jewish?"

"No."

"We used to have a cleaning woman whose name was Tessa. She was Jewish. From Poland."

"Cool."

"So you're not Jewish."

"No, I'm nothing."

"It's an original name for a Quebecer."

"It's a ruse."

"What?"

"A ruse."

Nico pretended he had to tie his shoelace and turned

his back on me. My mom had always said that sarcasm and irony are signs of intelligence. Maybe that was her way of making herself feel better about me. But she forgot to add that in Montreal in 1993, neither irony nor sarcasm worked with boys from the good neighbourhoods. At any rate, I wasn't interested in Nico. His hair did nothing for me, and I was sure he didn't play bass in a grunge band, whereas Raph and his band Sad Dolphin amped up our high-school dances; each band member had an engraved dolphin on his instrument case, Raph's dolphin was the most beautiful of all, and I had never been so head over heels in love.

Two dreadlocked college students stepped behind us with their cannabis-induced good humour and Hacky Sacks. They formed a circle with the Anglos and their game lasted for a good portion of the night. No one else showed up. Despite my excitement at the prospect of seeing Eddie Vedder and my determination to experience something exceptional, in all truth, that night outside was a real bore. I thought of the dog-eared page in my copy of *Wuthering Heights* waiting for me on my nightstand and I was sorry I hadn't brought it along. Sophie was smoking with the private-school boys, already friends; she peppered them with questions about everything—their lives, their parents, their travel plans, their cult movies, their favourite chocolate—and the already marked contrast between her luminosity and my shitload of gloom was blinding. Every two hours, I offered to make a run to Dunkin' Donuts next door for coffee. The second time, around four, Sophie came with me. "Olivier's falling for you," I pointed out. Sophie rolled her eyes and knit her brow, something only she can do, irresistibly so, meaning, *I don't agree, but I do agree, and I won't say so, but I like it.* It was genuine, everything about Sophie was genuine—her bravery, her loyalty, her goodness, her nonchalance, her pain, her pleasure. I had never had, never would have, a better friend. That she had chosen me to accompany her through her days, through the dull classes (which I quite liked actually), deliriously wacky parties (that terrified me), silent cottages (where I lay awake wide-eyed listening to her snore and thanking the heavens because hearing her next to me kept me from drowning in anxiety), that she had chosen me, me, when any of the other girls would have loved to be her best friend, was the greatest and most exquisite mystery of all. Sophie had stayed true to me from that very first day in high school when we ended up at the same cafeteria table. I offered her half my bag of Doritos, she asked if it was me who sang Ferré's "Avec le temps" at the choir audition. I stammered, embarrassed and ecstatic that a moment so pivotal in my mapping of the world lived on in someone else's memory. *Yeah, that was me. It was an idiotic choice.*

She told me the only idiotic thing was to talk about it that way; after that she listened to and loved John Lennon's tunes on my Walkman. "Woman Is the Nigger of the World." That's one that spoke to Sophie. I never thanked my brother for recording those songs in the exact order they were heard by Sophie that lunch hour in the cafeteria. In an act of generosity, Étienne had agreed to let me lend it to her, despite its being his favourite. I should have thanked him, because that tape was what brought Sophie to me and transformed my life.

Fortunately, my repeated doughnut-buying runs gave me an opportunity to loathe myself in peace. Despite all my usual tricks to discreetly avoid their joints, their gin, and their blotters, I was convinced they all *knew*. All you had to do was swallow something questionable in a dark place with loud music and you were cool. But I was always afraid. I was never cool. Sophie couldn't care less; she thought I was naturally funny, *You don't need anything else, you're already crazy.* Still, it was so lame, I was so lame, everyone knew. My heart pounded as I stared at the spread of cream-filled doughnuts. "Half a dozen or a dozen?" My ears rang, I couldn't hear anymore, I was about to faint, and the only thing that mattered was that it not happen in front of everyone else. I mumbled some feeble excuse, ran to the washroom and did the only thing my body demanded: I lay down on the floor, its tiles dirty but cold.

The cold eased my nausea. But not my fear of dying. It took several minutes of self-talk to bring myself down. *It's five in the morning, but even so, you're tired, yeah but, you ate too much sugar, that's true, you've had too much coffee, I always drink coffee, you're not having a heart attack, how do you know? You're just tired, maybe, you won't throw up, but what if, you're not going to die, you think so? You won't die, okay, you won't die.*

I'd experienced the same thing before, fleetingly, after eating a big piece of sugar pie, a sickness in the pit of my stomach that felt cataclysmic, like after a sleepless, anxiety-ridden night or the Chernobyl disaster or the kidnapping of that little boy in Hochelaga. But an end-of-the-world feeling like this one, that was a first. Then it too passed. My body settled into its natural rhythm. I held my finger to my wrist all the same, taking my pulse for what seemed like hours. When I returned to my spot by the campers carrying the box of doughnuts I'd managed to buy after the washroom incident *(if I can buy this boxful, that means I won't die)*, I had no trouble picking up my conversation with Sophie right where we'd left off.

"I'm just a fat, ugly girl with no future, let's be honest here. That's all I am."

"Don't be an idiot, Tess."

"No, but take a good, hard look. If you stick to scientific facts, it's all true."

"It's all false."

"You're just saying that because you're nice. And you're my friend."

"I'm saying that because it's true. You're being an idiot. Not fat, not ugly, and for sure not without a future. But idiotic."

"Idiotic ugly fat no future."

"Hold your tongue, woman."

When the sun rose over Sainte-Catherine, we were playing tic-tac-toe on my sleeping bag. I felt better. "I had some kind of blood pressure thing in that washroom, too many doughnuts," I said nonchalantly, testing the waters. Was I a good liar? If Sophie thought otherwise, she had enough class not to dig any deeper, and since Olivier had thrown up his 4 a.m. pizza in front of everyone else, I had no trouble giving him the sick prize and letting my episode go unmentioned.

Ten o'clock rolled around in no time. At dawn, the line grew longer and by the time the box office opened, it snaked down the street and around the corner almost to René-Lévesque. A bit shakily, Sophie and I pocketed our tickets and headed home. After a comatose nap of four to five hours, we called each other. I told her, "The whole show sold out in twenty-two minutes. Can you believe it? Twenty-two minutes!"

She said, "You see, good thing we were there!"

She knew, or maybe not, that our all-nighter out-doors was a heroic act on my part. Some link had been made, a sailor's knot tied between my heart and my feet, something like courage, and I would revel in the memory of my daring for weeks to come.

WE SHOULD HAVE LEFT early Friday instead, as Dad kept telling us while we baked in the back seat of his car. At the Lacolle border crossing, we'd been waiting in line for two hours already. He and Monique should have taken Friday off. Everyone knows that the first Saturday of the July construction holiday is a traffic nightmare. But her working conditions weren't the same as his. All morning, Monique kept saying, "Anyhow, Yves, if everyone had been ready for six thirty like they were supposed to be, customs would have been a breeze." I waited for her to finish her thought, forming the words in my head a few seconds before she uttered them, *Anthony and I were ready.*

Anthony, twelve, an only child, his forehead forever glistening, uncomfortable in his own skin, jerked his head away, as he did every time he was included in his mother's grousing, embarrassed by her lack of street smarts. He said nothing, but the angle of his neck gave him away, and Étienne and I shared a look. *She's too tough. He's too soft. Who cares?* I turned my attention to the hundreds of unmoving cars.

People came and went, some to the washrooms, others for a smoke break, others still to the Pepsi machine. I scanned the tide of pastel T-shirts and golf shorts, trying to spot, by some unlikely stroke of luck, Raph's family off for their holiday on the same day as us. But Raph probably didn't spend his summers on Maine's packed beaches. His parents collected books on the history of India and vegetarian cuisine, their living room was furnished with Moroccan poufs — not a single sofa, only poufs. They were probably in an ashram or a music camp. His family was undeniably cooler than mine.

In the front seat, Yves laid his hand on Monique's thigh. Monique and her *constant* singing along to the radio's soft-rock songs. Monique and her overpowering Anaïs Anaïs perfume. I thought of my mother, her expression when she buckled my bag after my dad's call at 7:15. *We're on our way, make sure you're ready.* Ever since Yves moved to Montreal, he'd been the one in charge of our holidays. I could see Paule again, leaning over my worn canvas suitcase, one of the leather straps held together with a safety pin. Her grey hair under the henna dye.

"What will you do while we're away?"

Paule's eyes sought out her coffee, sitting on the sideboard at the front door, as though to put off her answer.

"You already know. I'll be working."

Her words came accompanied by a sigh, the sigh of my mother's eternal fatigue, the sigh I heard wherever I went. Not that I could help. But I wanted to shout at her, *Go somewhere with your girlfriends, escape with a lover to Charlevoix, buy a plane ticket to Paris, charge it to your credit card, go alone if you have to, just go, please, whatever you do, don't work, not when your children are off to Wells, Maine, with their dad in a Camry reeking of perfume, not when everyone else in the world is entitled to have it all even when they make lame choices.*

I didn't say a word.

"Anyway, it'll be boring. Monique'll make us play minigolf again."

For a second, the desire to laugh shone in her eyes; I knew it, I saw it. She couldn't stand Miss Prissy's perfumes or her soft rock. The look switched to one of disappointment. For my mother, maliciousness was worse than tackiness. "Tessa, really, try harder."

Her words came back to me in the car just as I was about to insist on another radio station. I pulled out my Walkman and held out the left earbud to Étienne. Poor Anthony would be left with nothing, but I couldn't help that. Monique should buy him his own Walkman.

She'd promised our holidays would be exceptional. She already knew the Wells Seaside Cottages, having spent several summers there with her sisters and their children; in fact, we'd spend our evenings around the campfire with her nieces and nephews. The motel had a saltwater pool, it even had bikes for the guests.

What Monique called *exceptional*, she, who at Christmas gave me a New Kids on the Block vinyl pencil case, would not necessarily fit my definition of the word.

The only thing *seaside* about Wells Seaside Cottages was the name. The sea wasn't even visible from the cabins — you had to cross the highway to get there. My main holiday fantasy (me, consumed with thoughts of Raph, strolling alone along the beach, away from the glittering lights of a rustic cottage, our cottage) collapsed. We caught a glimpse of the beach as we crossed the village, a small strip of flattened sand on which thousands of burnt sunbathers lay high and dry among the beach umbrellas and trash from their coolers. No tide, other than that of bloated flesh. The promise of a charming cottage and adorable nieces and nephews was shattered as quickly as my romantic imaginings. Monique's nephews, two high-strung eleven-year-olds, both wore their hair in a rat's tail, yes, both of them. Her niece, a bit older than me, was a zealous Bon Jovi fan, as evidenced by the T-shirt she wore tied above her navel. Her veneration even pushed her to copy Jon's bouffant hairstyle. "It's got that hairspray crunch," I said to Étienne after the usual introductions as I watched her walk off. He glared to remind me how unfunny I was with my cheap shots and I grumbled; it was tough having a brother who was such a hippy.

After five days spent on the burning beach and as many nights of hot dogs, I had run out of alternative scenarios *(what if I stumble upon Raph's dad's car on my way to the gas station to buy Popsicles after supper? The door opens and my heart stops. Raph sets foot on the asphalt, I see the birthmark on his ankle, and he's charmed stunned caught off guard, and we say something like,* What a dump this place is! *He invites me to meet him behind his cottage on a private beach, and I sneak over when everyone's in bed, and Raph kneads my breasts behind a dune and starts to take my panties off,* Keep going, I want it, I've wanted it for so long, I want it so bad that I cry out in my sleep. *The pain would be exquisite. I'd carry a handful of sand from our dune away with me so as not to forget. The next day I'd call Sophie and wouldn't even brag, I'd be discreet and brimming with wonderful secrets, then Raph would phone,* I'll be waiting for you tonight, *and he'd really mean it.)*

Nothing happened, not love or a tan worthy of the name. We were leaving for home the next day, and I could hardly wait. That night, as on every other night, we crammed into the cottage belonging to Sonia—sister to Monique and mother to Bon Jovi, the girl Étienne managed to feel up because he didn't discriminate and Bon Jovi looked like she'd be into it. At this lowest of lows in my state of boredom, I couldn't blame him, although I did make fun of Anthony who, in his innocence, thought his cousin was busy teaching Étienne how to fish. So Étienne, Bon Jovi, Anthony, the two rat-tails, and I squeezed together in front of the TV set in Sonia's cottage for the Miss America broadcast on ABC, a station we didn't get at home, one my mom would never have let us watch. The adults were out having a cigarette by the fire.

In Bon Jovi's opinion, Miss Indiana's tan was too fake. "Miss Georgia's got such frog eyes. Wow, did you see Miss Texas's hair? Miss Utah is the best of a bad lot." "No, I like Miss Vermont better." "Miss Vermont? You're so granola, Étienne." I'd like to have spoken up for Miss Vermont, too, to back up my brother, but in actual fact, I was mesmerized by Miss Washington, a tall brunette, the irises of her eyes verging on mauve, so calm she resembled a statue. Miss Washington didn't say much—despite having the most beautiful voice of the lot, a warm, golden alto—but that was because anything she could say would have been superfluous. Who needs to hear from a millenia-old statue? "Anyone notice how all Miss Washington says is yes or no? I bet it's because they're the only words she knows," I blurted out.

102

After the brief burn caused by my own cruelty, I was safe. No one would ever guess that, deep down, I longed to be Miss Washington.

OUR MOTHER HAD WORKED all week, just as she'd said. Exhausted as we were by the drive from Wells and Monique's singalongs, she didn't subject us to a detailed account of her week and didn't have us talk about ours either. She asked if we were hungry, then served leftover roast chicken. It was covered in a honey-thyme rub, something Monique would have called *special*. It was good, of course. But only special if you'd never had anything else to eat before in your whole life. I wondered why Paule didn't pester us with questions about Monique or any of the women who'd preceded her. She must hate them all, mustn't she? She, too, would have enjoyed hearing about their major flaws, their prissy outfits and their tawdry jewellry. If she only knew that Renée, the woman just before Monique, used to wear barrettes to match her winter coat, and a purse to match her daughter's dress! Wasn't that incredible info?

"You know, Dad's girlfriend doesn't think you should drink anything cold out of a cup."

"That's her choice."

"Get a load of this, she'd never heard of tortellini before!"

"You just found out what gelato is."

"But I'm only fifteen!"

"That doesn't give you the right to be rude."

A stone wall. My mother never played the game. Maybe she let loose with her friends, together tearing to shreds the women who'd taken their places with the men they'd cleaned up after through university and into their mid-thirties. Well within her rights to be pissed off, with her friends my mother again became the Gorgon I knew her to be. Maybe.

I THOUGHT I MIGHT borrow something of my mother's to wear to Hannah's party. I didn't know Hannah; she was a friend of Mandy's, the only Anglo in the class. Hannah lived in Westmount and her parents taught medicine at McGill. That brief bio was intimidating enough; to have Mandy point out that Hannah had a "huge fucking mansion of a house" when she issued the invite did nothing to calm my nerves. How could I show up without giving away my inner working-class girl straight from Petite-Patrie and my inability to be gracious and graceful too? "Tessa's a pretty name, but there's nothing else remotely ballerina-like about you!" snickered Chantal, the director of the ballet school I went to for half a session in grade four. What stuck with me was my incurable lack of finesse and taste of bitterness at a first name that didn't keep its promises. When I told Paule what Chantal had said, she was livid, grabbing the phone to tear a strip off the culprit, adding that the only thing the teacher's name "brings to mind is the kind of dancer you'd see inside a cage on the teen show *Jeunesse d'aujourd'hui.*"

That show hadn't aired for ages by then, but Chantal had to have grasped my mother's meaning—she was a dancer lacking in class—and for a woman so proud to teach modern dance to little girls, the remark was an obvious insult. I was overcome with pride and shame— we never mentioned the incident again, and I never asked to take dance again either.

Mandy was our ticket into Montreal's Anglophone world. She knew everyone west of Atwater, not to mention all the names of the comedians on *Saturday Night Live.* She liked Buddy Holly and Patsy Cline and had already sung karaoke in a bar in Nashville, Tennessee. With her Jane Birkin–ish accent, Mandy called us Sophie, *l'intrépide* and Tessa, *la tordue,* the bold and the twisted. She shone to the tips of her platinum hair, and Sophie and I adored her. It was unthinkable for me to show up in front of Mandy and her friends—surely as magical as she—in poor girl or, worse yet, good girl clothes. My mother's closet wasn't well-stocked. Her single state and thirty-plus years had thickened her waist, but she did have a few interesting vests, including a men's cut in a houndstooth motif that she sewed from modified patterns. The girls in *Singles* wore the same kind of thing: flowery dresses topped with a man's vest and workmen's boots, and *Singles* was a good movie, wasn't it? Hadn't Mandy said she liked it? Really, who hadn't liked *Singles*? Even Eddie Vedder had a role. What about adding a burgundy felt hat? Paule had a small one that lay forgotten in the front hall closet; it didn't quite fit my look, it was cloche-shaped and reminiscent of the twenties, but if I took out the feather she'd added, it would do. Sophie had been waiting at the Rosemont metro station for fifteen minutes by the time I arrived wearing my dress and boots, a vest under my arm, but no hat because, really, not everyone has it in them to be Bridget Fonda. The upshot was that I was a barely improved version of myself compared to any other day of the year. She embraced me effusively, kept saying, "I love your dress!" As for Sophie, she wore her usual uniform: jeans, espadrilles, and a sailor stripe top. Sophie in a dress was a rare and unsettling event, but whatever she wore, she always carried herself like a queen. *When you've got it, you've got it and Sophie's got it*, I used to sing to the tune of the France Gall song *Ella, Elle L'a*. She'd say *enough already* and I'd ignore her.

As soon as we got to Hannah's, it was clear we were dealing with an entirely different race of human being. The guests may have looked like us (a few ballcaps, a lot of Converse runners, two or three retro army jackets, and a set of dreadlocks), the music was the same as anywhere else (on our arrival, "Groove Is in the Heart"; by evening's end, "No Woman, No Cry"), and the liquor smelled like the punch we spiked at school dances. The difference was that everything took place in a huge mansion on white marble floors. Large windows covered one whole living room wall or, at least, the part of that room we had access to, and French doors led to a *Better Homes and Gardens* garden. A staircase took up a good part of the entranceway and spiralled upward to the bedroom floor. Hannah's bedroom, which Mandy led us to on our arrival, was as big as my living room at home. Her bed: a canopy bed. Posters of her idols: framed. Hannah herself gave no clue as to her social class. Only a few niceties showed her wealth: tiny diamond earrings and well-manicured nails. A subtle perfume wafted from her, evocative of lemons and rosemary. There was no way it could have come from a Jean Coutu drugstore. I tried to remember if I'd put on any deodorant before leaving; if not, my synthetic dress would be far from forgiving. I decided to wait until I was alone in the bathroom ("double-paned shower and gold faucets") to check my armpits. Hannah greeted us warmly, albeit in sketchy French. No problem—the insane number of hours I'd spent in front of American TV shows had done wonders for my English, and I jumped at the opportunity to show off. *Nice room! Awesome outfit! This party rocks!* The way I saw it, knowing the expressions used by real people — or at least, by teens in American sitcoms — was of the utmost importance.

Hannah offered us a joint, which Sophie happily accepted. I pretended to take a toke, which led to a full twenty minutes of self-monitoring, *is my heart racing, am I sweating, I feel dizzy, it's so hot, I'll be okay, but boy I really am sweating, I'll take off my boots, the cold'll do me good, thank God for cool marble floors, okay, no, everything's okay, you didn't even inhale, chill out, you weirdo,* during which I only half listened to the conversation. In a framed picture on Hannah's bedside table, I caught a glimpse of a woman, a brunette, in the sun, squinting to look at whoever was taking the picture, already delighted to see it's her beloved daughter.

Two cooing redheads, one tall, the other fat, walked in and dragged Hannah back downstairs. "Jon C. just showed up with Jon B., oh my God, Hannah, where's my gloss!"

"That's her mother."

"She looks like her."

Mandy leaned closer and mouthed, "She died last spring. Ovarian cancer."

I looked again at the nightstand, at the woman without a single grey hair, young despite her motherly outfit (a flowered La Cache dress, straw hat, designer jewellry), and felt an urgent need to know when the picture had been taken. Had she known she was ill that day and what awaited her? Did she smile for her daughter because she knew that smile would outlast her? Did she rail against the atrocity of death, her face smothered in her pillow at night? Did she feel that forty-some years was acceptable for one lifetime? To comfort Hannah near the end, did she tell her daughter that she'd had a rich, beautiful, full, *sufficient* life? And if so, how could she truly believe that? Maybe mothers tell lies on their deathbeds.

"How long ago was the picture taken?"

"Dunno. Come see, there's a patio on the roof."

Mandy got up from the bed and motioned for us to follow her. Sophie hooked her pinkie into mine. *Get out of your head.*

I DIDN'T SLEEP OVER at Sophie's as planned that night. At ten past midnight, I pretended I had to catch the last train and fled. Sophie didn't insist. She knew my need to be alone, I knew her desire to get the hell out, and *don't get in the way* was the motto that summed up our friendship.

At forty-eight past midnight, after an endless metro ride peopled with drunks and hockey fans, I opened the door to our house. Étienne wasn't home yet. That summer, sometimes we'd cross paths only once or twice a week. He was about to start college, and then we'd see even less of him. That was the way it was.

The door to Paule's bedroom stood open. She lay fast asleep under her thick handmade quilt, the one I so loved when I was little with its gold piping and large squares of raspberry silk charmeuse. Her still outline reminded me of the children's book I'd read so often about the owl frightened by the shape of its own feet under the covers. Her breathing was loud and slow, regular and deep, its rhythm occasionally broken by a little snore. The minutes ticked by on the clock by her bed.

Fifty past midnight. Sunk in her bed, my mother was immense and tiny and so alone. At the door sat a pair of old running shoes flecked with green, blue, and yellow, the ones she wore to paint in. A pair of socks was stuffed into one of the runners. She'd begun painting an old church pew she'd scavenged from a friend's garage; that was how she'd spent her day. I wanted to wake her up, tell her about Hannah's mother, tell her she had to live forever. I would never be ready to let her go. I'd promise to help her paint the pew on Sunday. We could go for ice cream afterwards and, most of all, I'd tell her that no one was stronger than she was.

I didn't though. It was the middle of the night and, anyhow, we weren't a sentimental kind of family.

Tomorrow

"I can't guarantee it, but I'm almost sure it gave her a thrill."

"She's despicable, we've known that for a long time."

"She literally said, 'Aww.' As in *Aww . . . poor you.*"

"Like I said, despicable."

"She said, 'Aww . . . I don't know how you do it. I'd die if I didn't have children.'"

"Stupid idiot."

"She wasn't trying to be mean."

"I'm sure she wasn't trying to be a stupid idiot either, but she is one."

"Who does that? Who says that to someone who's just had a miscarriage, goddammit!"

"I'm so sorry, Sophie."

"You're such a sweetheart."

"Have you two decided what's next?"

"Not yet. I've never liked the idea of a clinic, you

know that. Maybe I've waited too long."

"Do you want me to give you one of mine? That is a possibility."

"They'd miss you too much."

"That bloody bitch should eat shit."

"You bet."

"Not to mention that book of hers, pure drivel."

"Did you read it?"

"Leafed through it in the store. You've never read anything as self-indulgent or embarrassing. In an interview, she called it a *momvel*. Seriously! You wouldn't want to be her."

"I don't want to be her."

"You wouldn't want her husband either."

"Shit no."

"'Mr. Hard-on'?"

"He really lets her write that on her blog?"

"It's 'cause he gets such hard-ons. Not."

Sophie's laugh.

"I tell you Sophie, the more someone goes on about their great life with Mr. Hard-on, the fishier it sounds, everyone knows that. Mr. Soft-on. Mr. Anti-Hard-on."

"Thanks, Tess. It's not her fault that she's got kids."

"It's entirely her fault. The problem is she thinks kids appear as if by magic to those who truly deserve them. When the truth is she's just plain vulgar and has hyperactive ovaries, like me."

"You're no vulgar hyperactive ovarian."

"Nothing is less certain."

"You're such an idiot."

"Got time for lunch?"

"No, I've got a million things to do."

"Shall we go anyway?"

"You bet."

THE FOUR OF THEM left early, all in a rush to give Philémon enough time to zip through the math homework he'd forgotten in his locker. His forgetfulness earned him his mother's ire and then an extra cookie in his lunchbag because of the guilt brought on by the motherly ire. Up since six, Boris and Oscar were happy to follow their father. Neither knew the morning blues, a quality they inherited from Jim, who loves his sons as he loves his wife and life itself—boldly and with fierce resolve.

The minute the door closes is usually one I cherish. It's like when you wave a teatowel under a smoke detector and, after all the chaos and running around, the alarm finally stops. You're left alone in the silence, your hair a mess. Today, the calm that prevails seems out of place, almost scandalous. My time is mine for a few hours before my lunch with Sophie; then I'll accompany a couple in their forties to see a house on Île Bizard, I'll pick up the children at school, and we'll crowd the narrow entrance with our shoes and spring jackets. I'm alone, and what is normally a luxury and a well-deserved treat (if you go by all those yogurt and chocolate bar ads) is filled with foreboding. Is this my life from here on in? Once I've destroyed our world, will I keep waking up to this mute indifference?

A Montreal spring, exuberant and unambiguous, is cruel for the unhappy among us. Everyone is wound up in the spring in Montreal; we are a herd returning to pasture after winter. During our seasonal retreat, only the flu bug makes it into our sealed shelters. Upon our release, the gates are thrown open, we're flooded with sap and hope, and everyone knows too well that hope is never more heart-wrenching than for those of us who are sad. Those who venture outdoors risk even greater disappointment, face to face with those of us who are happy: *Why don't you try just a little? Go outside, the patios are open!* So for the most part during Montreal's spring, the unhappy among us keep our mouths shut and bob our heads like those car ornaments, the bobbleheads, taunting us during traffic jams. There is nothing sadder than being sad when you're the only one.

Looking for the outdoor café Sophie suggested for our meeting, I see among the seated diners — laughing, blustering, whispering, and chattering — a sad-eyed contingent. The man who barely takes time to sit down before ordering a beer. The woman whose gaze flits from one to another of her colleagues, her lips pressed together. The boy on a skateboard nearby, a taller version of Philémon, who never looks up, just keeps trying the same tricks over and over. Sophie, sitting in a secluded corner of the patio in the shade, her cheek resting on her balled-up fist, asking herself the same questions over and over: *Will I ever have children? What if I don't?* For Sophie, there's no question about where she belongs.

"Nice day out. I hate it."

Sophie hears my voice and looks up with a smile. At some point between the long-gone days when we watched boys playing basketball in the schoolyard and today, she saw darkness descend on me. I'd call it *lucidity* since that's the right word and one doesn't exclude the other, but people don't like to think their life won't fulfill the promises made in the cradle or around the fire when they shone as only adolescents can, driven by the unshakeable certainty that *everything will be fine.* I was once like them.

Sophie doesn't age. She works, talks, laughs, sleeps a lot, sometimes travels. But she doesn't age. You might think it's because she's worn the same uniform for the past twenty years, her runners and sailor stripe tops, her discreet European grace, her dark bob—but that's not it. The reason Sophie doesn't age is she doesn't know how. Which doesn't mean she can't be in a bad mood occasionally.

"That's true, it is a nice day out."

It's something worth pointing out, both for her and for me.

"Also true that I hate it."

124

Spoken aloud, things take on real contours and are revealed in all their absurdity. Is it that implacable logic that leads me to say nothing to Sophie? A hundred minutes spent on the restaurant terrace together and none of them devoted to talk of Francis. We order, eat, laugh even more over Ms. Momvel, Sophie's journalist colleague from a few years ago, her small-ish literary success and her lame book recounting the adventures of a mother blessed with four children (a boy, twin girls, another boy). Sophie is too classy to mock her openly, so I take up the baton with unabashed pleasure. Of course, my hostility is ugly and reeks of bitterness, but I'm on Sophie's side and hold nothing back.

So why not say a single word about Francis?

Sophie knows everything about the man, from how much I've missed him to how that weighed me down. She knows about the years spent looking for him everywhere, in songs, in movies, in the thousands of steps taken on the sidewalks of my city. She knows that Jim knows next to nothing about that time because, for many years, even the mention of his name hurt. She knows everything. What I said, and what I didn't say. She knows what hasn't healed.

So. Why not mention Francis?

Maybe because I can guess that, despite our friendship and years of shared secrets, or maybe because of them, she wouldn't believe — in either Francis's steadfastness or my resolve. The light veil of disapproval that would drop down over her big blue eyes would only be a reflection of my own. I couldn't stand that because, whatever the cost, I need something to relieve the grief I've been drunk on for years now. Hasn't Francis resurfaced to sober me up? Knowing as much, how can I deprive myself?

Tomorrow will be another nice day. The fourth consecutive day with clear skies. I could bring out the gold ballerina flats I bought off the Internet in a moment's madness last summer and that I've only worn for a grand total of three times because the sight of my woman's feet in young girl's shoes sickened me. I stored them at the back of the closet with the swimsuits. But tomorrow will be no ordinary day. The circumstances call for gold flats and a new dress; it's a day to defy all conventions, a day to once again meet the man-who-changed-everything-and-revealed-me-to-myself. A woman in the throes of passion no longer has to comply with age or status-based rules, right? She becomes Charlotte Gainsbourg on the streets of Paris, Patti Smith in a recording session, or Emily Brontë taking charge of her own education. She's free.

On Villeray on my way back from my lunch with

Sophie, I spot a dress in a store window. Klein blue fabric, dotted with grey stars so tiny they look like grains of sand. I step inside, grab the dress without trying it on. It has to fit, it will fit, I buy it. The salesclerk wraps the dress in tissue paper, I almost say *no, no need, I'll be wearing it tomorrow.* But I let her. I can. For the pleasure of unwrapping it tonight, then hanging it in the closet, hidden between two real estate agent blouses.

When I step outside with my little black bag, I follow two girls in T-shirts, their round thighs encased in leggings, laughing and singing a current pop hit, bouncy and light, even the chubbier of the two. *Don't they have a class to go to?* would be my usual thought, but today I'm not their mother; I'm freedom and confidence. I'm their eyes alight with the future.

A rare occurrence.

One whispers into the other's ear and both burst into flustered, triumphant laughter. They speak of the sacred, the salacious; they are wonderful and I smile so hard tears fill my eyes.

Then the phone rings. The girls' heads swivel; they see me staring and hurry away. My intensity sent chills down their spine. *If a grown-up stares at you with a strange look in their eye, make a run for it. (Yes, the grown-up can be a woman.)*

The phone keeps on ringing. I have to rummage through my purse, find it at the very bottom, answer.

"Do you have a couple of minutes?"

"I. Yes. How are you, Évelyne?"

"Oh..."

"Évelyne..."

"I shouldn't, we really don't know each other."

"No, that's true. That's very true."

"But I'm going to say it anyway."

"Of course."

"I slept with someone in Toronto."

"..."

"Do you think I'm shameless?"

"..."

"Tessa?"

"You slept with someone in Toronto?"

"A colleague. I thought he was good-looking, we'd bump into each other at seminars, but I never thought... We had sex all night!"

"That's. That's marvellous, Évelyne."

"That's not all."

"...No?"

"No. He's coming to Montreal at the end of the week. He wants us to get together."

"Oh. Is that all?"

"Pardon me?"

"Was that all you wanted to say? Nothing else?"

"I. No, why?"

"Nothing. That's perfect. He wants to see you again."

"Should I?"

"You should do whatever you feel like doing."

"He kissed every last inch of me. He told me ten, maybe a hundred times, how fabulous I was. Then he was ready to start all over again twenty minutes later. The next morning too. He texted me all day long. Nothing too serious though. Jokes, code words. He said, 'Any guy who lets you get away is crazy.' What do you think I feel like doing?"

"So then, do it. Do it. Who's there to stop you?"

"Nobody. Especially not Francis."

A blow, an absence. An attack of tachycardia. *It's normal for her to say his name.*

"No. You're right."

"By the way, he told me you'd seen each other."

"What?"

"Francis told me he was there at the house when you stopped by."

"That's what he told you."

"Yes. He thought you looked qualified."

"Ha!"

"What? Does that seem condescending? It is a bit condescending. Francis can be very paternalistic. Robert says that—Robert is my . . . I suppose he's my lover, isn't he? Robert says paternalism is the weapon of the weak."

" . . . "

"I've talked about him too much. Not a good thing."

"No worries."

"Perhaps I should put a stop to it all. What if he gets bored? The humiliation. I couldn't."

"Yes."

"Yes?"

"No, I meant yes, I understand. Not yes, you should put a stop to it."

"But am I right to be wary?"

"Évelyne, about the house. I may have a problem."

"Oh?"

"Yes. Some infighting at the office. We've been asked to work as a team."

"What does that change?"

"It means my team partner sees Ahuntsic as her territory. She wants to look after you."

"No!"

No was right. Back at the office, Guylaine would be delighted to share a listing with me, but no one has forced my hand. Yet it's the only thing I can think of right then to put some distance between me and Évelyne.

"I don't want someone else!"

"I'm so sorry. She'll be responsible for most of the showings. I promise that won't change a thing for your house."

"I know. I'm being ridiculous. It's just that I'd thought we might be friends."

WHEN I WAS FIRST with Jim, both of us smoked. He liked his morning cigarette over coffee in our apartment's miniscule kitchen. The air grew thick with smoke; we had to open the door, its thousand shades of the same grey, cracked, crooked, with panes of glass so old they looked frosted. The sunlight that did manage to filter through set plumes of dust to dancing. I don't know why the memory of all that dirt is dear to me, but it is. I always liked smoking at night better, when the only perceptible light came from the tip of the cigarette I'd just taken a drag from, lighting up then going dark like a torso rising and falling with each breath.

After Philémon's birth, we spaced out the sharing of cigarettes. Jim began to feel he couldn't play his instrument as well as before, so he quit. I soon followed because with Boris's then Oscar's birth, the masquerade became laughable. Who is this old mother sitting cross-legged and smoking in her toy-strewn backyard? Not me. No longer me.

But I never got out of the habit of heading out to the yard when the weather warmed up, once the boys went to bed. Tonight the temperature's mild, and anyway, no one wants to shut themselves up like a mummy. There's no way I can stay inside next to Jim in front of the TV set watching fictional people go through their traumas in order to remind us how lucky we are, *Aren't we lucky, honey?* I don't have a cigarette, but I did open a bottle of white wine; it's Thursday, and I've brought my glass out with me.

"The stars'll be out."

Behind the wooden fence, my neighbour points at the sky. I forget that it's not just birds and buds that come out in the springtime—neighbours do too.

"Evening, Roland."

"There's still too much light, but come eleven o'clock or midnight, they'll be out."

"That's what you say, but they can't be seen in the city."

"With my telescope they can."

Roland puts his eye to the lens again, his back hunched over. Soon he's groaning in discomfort, but he doesn't change his position.

"Would you like me to adjust the height?"

"Huh?"

"Your telescope. It's too low for you, Roland."

"I like it this way."

"But it hurts, I can hear you."

"It's perfect just the way it is. It's at Rosa's height."

Rosa, Roland's wife, didn't make it through the winter. She died on New Year's Day, just after a visit from their grandson, Nathan, who's enrolled in military college.

No one thought she'd survive till spring. She huffed like a locomotive and her oxygen tank followed her everywhere. Roland would wheel her into the yard on clear summer evenings so she could admire the Big Dipper. *Three packs of Player's a day for forty-seven years*, he proclaimed when she died, not without a certain amount of pride. His Rosa never bowed to anything.

"The kids think I should sell. They say I'm sitting on a goldmine."

"You'd get six hundred thousand for it, maybe six-fifty."

"We paid forty-two thousand in 1974. Poor young people."

He shakes his head and rubs his neck, not too conspicuously, but still: he hurts all over and has ever since she's been gone.

When I close the sliding door to the kitchen on my way inside, the house is plunged into silence. The lightbulbs in the hood above the stove produce a weak pool of light. Everything is so familiar. The subway tile I still congratulate myself for choosing, despite the crumbling grout. The open shelves, a great idea stolen from six-year-old decorating magazines, shelves that actually turned out to be disastrous — pots, cake pans, sieves, lids, rolling pins idly gather dust (I quit sorting them into pretty colour-coded piles a long time ago). On the jatoba hardwood floor, bought on sale and laid by Jim one ambitious Sunday (the result is pleasing but the grooves are too loose, it will never qualify as a "professional" job), crumbs of bread, rice crackers, and parmesan forever accumulate no matter how often it's swept. The empty sink shines. The walls, victims of my obsession with grey three years ago, have taken on the colour of a raincloud. I still like it. But the colour bleeds in places onto the white moulding that needs repainting. That's when I'll fill the holes left by the finishing nails, my finger dirty with latex.

Those jobs are the kind I like, repetitive and satisfying, with guaranteed results.

The dining room is cloaked in darkness. Its table is never totally uncluttered. Philémon's science and geography quizzes lie waiting for our signature. He must have left them there once he'd finished his homework. I can't find a pen; I'll have to remember them tomorrow. I examine Philemon's earnest but messy handwriting, his stellar grades, from day one. Boris is not as lucky, but his penmanship is divine.

By late evening, the room looks austere, detached from the rest of the house. The built-in china cabinet, as old as the gypsum walls, still sports its porcelain handles. Jim has often suggested repainting its oak white to brighten the room, and I almost said yes. I'm usually not a purist for the natural look; it's something I often say to clients, mouldings have been repainted since time immemorial, you shouldn't let a house go for so little. Yet I never could get used to the idea in my own dining room.

I sometimes sit here sewing on buttons, mending torn knees and eviscerated stuffies. We don't have a hearth, but I play the Victorian anyway and find the shadows strangely companionable. This dark isn't afraid of my own darkness.

Oscar has abandoned his clothes on the bathroom floor. His pants and small socks, miniscule versions of a man's clothes, lie scrunched on the mat. As usual, the pirate boat and goggles are left out. There is a cupboard for storing toys, and a laundry hamper in the corner by the washstand. But here life overflows more than in the other rooms. Not that I can talk. My creams and nail polishes, now thick and unuseable, bought in the lame hope of transforming my soul, the hairbrushes that, when purchased, promised to *change my life*, lie heaped on the counter. I simply drop the clothes in the hamper.

From the very first day, the living room has been the heart of the home. Since our arrival, we've removed the columns characteristic of the 1920s building style, then the doors and a long stretch of wall just before Boris was born. We baptized that period "the epic renovation of 2006." Once the living room was gutted, we dug the basement to welcome the hockey nets and Ping-Pong table a future of young boys held in store for us. "Guaranteed added value," Sylvain often said at the office, thoroughly convinced that heaven was having an eight-foot ceiling and stainless steel appliances. As expected, our basement is strewn with abandoned knick-knacks, robots made of boxes covered in tinfoil, and every size of children's clothing from zero to eleven

crammed into more-or-less organized bins. Every time
I head down with another load for the laundry, I wonder
why I insist on keeping them all. Boris, sturdier than
his big brother, wears almost the same size despite the
two-year age difference. Oscar could use the big boys'
clothes, but by the time they reach him, they're torn
and stained and I reuse very few. No one will ever wear
the clothes in the "zero to three" and "three to five"
bins. Wouldn't they be better off in the hands of some
underprivileged children somewhere east of where I
live, rather than here feeding the raging nostalgia that
inhabits me? Maybe I'll be able to give them away later.
Once the storm has passed, and all the tough conversations and fighting are over, once Jim and I are left
vanquished and empty, it will be easy to give away
those bins of clothes. *Bet your bottom dollar*, I think all
of a sudden as I turn off the basement light — the boys
always forget — and then a song comes to me, the one
little Annie sings in the '70s musical comedy that Oscar
watched again and again over the Christmas holiday.
*The sun'll come out tomorrow / Bet your bottom dollar that
tomorrow / There'll be sun.* It's not hard to leave, not
when you have somewhere to go. We're always leaving
something or someone behind. How many clients have
I seen agonizing over the decision to sell the house in
which their children were born, only to jump eagerly
at the first attractive offer? I've driven Jim to the airport

so many times before a tour, watching the lightness in his step as he walked away from us, like that of a teen tasting freedom. Why wouldn't I be able to walk away just as easily from everything I've known, everything that belongs to me and carries my trace?

Aren't I entitled to that sun *tomorrow*? If I called my brother to ask for his advice, he'd laugh, take a drag off his cigarette, and sing, *It's the end of the world as we know it, and I feel fine.* He'd be his usual non-judgemental hippy self. But I won't be calling Étienne. Étienne died over fifteen years ago.

2004

MOST SURPRISING OF ALL was how clearly I perceived sound. Only the baby's squeals interrupted the gratifying silence in the apartment. When he slept, infinitely heavy in my arms despite his feather weight, I could hear the hum of the fridge intensify at the opposite end of the kitchen and the rustling of pages as my mother, seated in the living room, sat reading a Swedish thriller and waiting for my instructions: change the baby, take the baby, rock the baby, make the next meal. "Pretend I'm not here unless you need help." She was on holiday — a lucky coincidence — when Philémon was born and had all the time in the world. She put herself at our disposal with no strings attached from the second Philémon emitted his first pint-sized giant cry, one July night, in a hospital in the east of the city. En route to the hospital, just before midnight, the radio announced Reggiani's death. Jim took it as a good sign:

his son, too, would be a musician. My mother begged, "Promise me you won't call him Serge. Life brings enough hardships of its own without that." I didn't need to ask what she meant. For the past four years, our combined lives revolved around the same dark sun. Étienne died after a fall from a tall cliff one May morning in Scotland, during a trip with friends, a last hurrah together before scattering to their adult lives, one with a science education degree, another an industrial design degree, another, like Étienne, with a not-quite finished degree in cinema, "but nine credits are nothing, by Christmas I'll have it." His friends returned home horror stricken, carrying their missing companion's backpack. They gave it to my parents as though it were a relic. It took over ten days to repatriate his body. An eternity.

Étienne's friends proved to be generous with us. My parents asked them to tell the story of the last days, his last hours, until his friends were blue in the face. They were always game and treated each time as if it was the first, embellishing their accounts here and there to flesh out the story, to do some good so that Étienne might live a little longer, even if only in the world of storytelling.

"'I've never seen anything as beautiful as Rowardennan in my life,' were his words on our arrival. Our youth hostel was beautiful too, an old stone house, almost a manor, it even had a turret. I'll show you the pictures once they're developed. From our room, we could see Loch Lomond and a mountain in the distance. It was just so perfect, we decided to stay on. There was a group of Italian girls, they were really fun. Étienne had his eye on one of the four, Valeria, tall with curly hair. They spent all three evenings outside by the fire telling stories and drinking beer. The last night they stayed outdoors till morning. Étienne joined us for breakfast, wearing a smile as big as the moon. Valeria had given him her address, said we could visit her when we were in Italy. She'd fallen in love like that, in just one night. Not that I'm surprised. Étienne always had that effect on girls. It really bugged us. The next morning we started out for the West Highlands Way—I'd read good things in my guidebook about the Devil's Staircase, a steep path but not all that dangerous if you stuck to it. We planned to go to Italy afterwards. We wanted to see Scotland, Ireland, London, Paris, Marseilles, Italy, Greece. Oh, Étienne wanted to go to the Cyclades too. In the end, all we saw was the Amsterdam airport, the Glasgow airport, Glasgow's pubs, cars driving on the left between lochs, the Rowardennan village, then the devil's mountain itself. Leaving the hospital, Fred was bawling like a calf, saying over and over, 'If it had happened at the end of the trip instead, at least Étienne could have known other countries too.' But the thing is, Étienne was thrilled with things as they were. That's what he said in Rowardennan, 'I've never seen anything as beautiful in my life. We can die happy, guys.' Then he laughed and opened another beer. It was just an off-the-cuff remark. But thinking back to that moment, it makes your blood run cold."

My parents listened to the bitter end of Christophe's story, nodding, squeezing their eyes shut from time to time, interrupting him at the same spots again and again to ask the same questions. My mother: "Did you take a picture of Valeria? I'd like to see her." My dad: "Was it Guinness he drank? He liked those dark beers, eh?" Paule and Yves, reunited in the same room, were only one of many surreal scenes I'd witness over the days following my brother's death. The presence of my father, in a tracksuit, seated in Paule's old overstuffed armchair where I'd seen her spend evenings reading and sewing, watching TV and talking on the phone, seemed both improbable and natural to me. This is what happens when death comes to call: the unknown becomes so brutally familiar that nothing shocks you anymore. There's a period of détente — a horrific one, of course — in the gravity-free state that confers on the bereaved a kind of as yet untapped power.

I surprised myself thinking several times a day, *This would be something to tell Francis. Francis would laugh at this. Francis would be moved by my tears.* I wanted to phone him; despite the eight months of silence between us I'd convinced myself that, *Hey, if ever there was a good reason to call him, this is it.* But his number had changed, and he wasn't in the phone book. Between our breakup and Étienne's death, a new century had begun, but nothing else had changed. Francis, too, had disappeared, and his absence, even in the fever of grief, only served as a reminder of that fact: he was all I could think of.

ON THE MORNING OF Étienne's funeral, his friends worked hard to put together a quick collage of Christophe's pictures that was displayed on an easel by the coffin in the funeral home. I thought they might have been too much. Even though my parents wanted to see the photos, it was not the best time to impose the last images of their son on them; it seemed indecent somehow, too in-your-face. Wasn't this death inherently theirs? Were they not the legitimate heirs? Did they feel no jealousy toward the boy-men with their greasy hair (except at the funeral! What a sight, every head of usually grubby hair shining on this day, bathed in the sunlight coming through the church's stained glass window, all the weeping young men whose resemblance to children had been revived by just one quick shampoo; I joked about it discreetly with Sophie during the reception buffet afterwards), hadn't they stolen from them their last moments with Étienne? The man who had wanted this child, the woman who bore him and nursed him, the parents who watched him grow, had calmed his moods, mopped up his vomit, suffered through his homework and the apathy of adolescence, to then be deprived of their son's last days of happiness, *Never seen anything as beautiful in my life*, only receiving from him, ten days before his death, a bungled good-bye, a quick hug at the Montreal airport surrounded by traffic officers reminding them to *Please keep moving, you can't park in the departure lane,* this man and this woman should not have had to put up with shared farewells.

But no. Yves and Paule were delighted by the pictures, delighted to have Étienne's friends there, touched, like them, by the footprints Étienne had left on the world. My parents preferred portioning out Étienne (with his friends, with the Italian girl, with the manager of the youth hostel, if it came to that) to owning him outright. In grief, they had lost the notion of ego itself; they were engulfed in pure love with none of the harshness of the living. It took me a long time, probably until Philémon's birth, to grasp even fleetingly what love was made of. Unlike them, I spent those years lost in introspection, measuring the effect life had had on me—Étienne's glaring absence, only rivalled by that of Francis, then mitigated by Jim's arrival and Philémon's birth. Four long years in the painful vortex of the most absolute egotism. Still. I would have liked to believe that, with Philémon's entry into the world in 2004, I was healed of my hypervigilance, of the pathetic passion for navel-gazing—for a while, I did believe that was the case. I lost the obsessiveness, of course, Philémon's life becoming infinitely more important to me, more essential than my own, which was an immense relief. But I had only to see my mother with the baby, her lighthearted repetition of gestures, the wonderful eclipse of expectations (*He exists, I saw him arrive, what a privilege, Tessa*), to understand how far from detachment I really was. I was nothing but love and torment.

OUR APARTMENT TOOK UP the north half of the second floor of a five-suite building in the heart of Saint-Denis traffic, on the Plateau where all my friends lived and that still had a student-worker-bourgeois feel. It resembled the apartments we hung out in: faded moulding repainted twenty times, thin maple slats of flooring warped by time and the clay soil, rooms in a row, and so much space given over to hallways. Before Philémon, I'd never noticed the hallways before. But over the first few weeks of his life, I spent so many hours walking ours that I came to know them like the moles on my arms. Here, an inactive phone jack. There, the original wall light fixtures to which I'd added tiny department store shades that I adorned with ribbon embroidered with orange beads in a stab at decorating, a stab at accomplishing something other than eating and sleeping over the long weeks during which I had nothing to do but wait on Philémon. Farther down were Jim's boxes of vinyl, hundreds of records that, one day, would have their own cabinet. He planned to build one as soon as we had enough money for good wood. Meanwhile, the records lived in green milk crates and took up half the hallway leading to the bathroom. I knew the boxes' contours by heart and never bumped into a single one.

With Philémon, every night was the same in a different way. His first cry jerked me out of the light damp sleep that had become my norm, and I'd sit on the edge of the bed, waiting to get to my feet. At first, Jim followed me to the baby's Moses basket, brought me glasses of water and the remote control and stayed near at hand as I nursed. Soon enough, I stopped waking him up. What was the point? Philémon and I had our routine.

I scooped the baby out of his basket, stood feeling his weight on my shoulder, then carried him into the living room. I could have stayed in bed to nurse him. Should have, if the brochures—all sweetness and light—given to us as we left the hospital were to be believed. But I liked the living room better. There, Philémon and I could go about our vital business: nursing, in his case, and watching reruns of home reno shows in mine. In the blessed silence, no interference. No guilt either. No criticism aimed at me for not doing something more important. No one to dare hint, through seemingly innocent questions, that having a baby was no career choice. *When are you going back to university? They have daycares, you know.* No, in the space we inhabited, there were only two people in perfect harmony and the scent of breast milk.

I was nothing but love and torment. And had been ever since Étienne's death. Maybe even ever since Francis left. Or maybe forever.

At first, I thought suffering would make me a better singer. Hadn't I chosen *Lamento d'Arianna* to audition for my bachelor's in music? *Lasciatemi morire*, that I cater-wauled with feeling. And it worked; I was accepted into the program. Now that I knew despair up close, I would become Monteverdi's most sensitive interpreter since Anne Sofie von Otter. But I hadn't factored in the stage fright I suffered every time I performed during my third year, either as part of the chorus or as a soloist, whether the repertory was just a Christmas carol for sick kids or the Purcell aria that would decide my final mark.

"Dido's Lament" in *Dido and Aeneas* reigned supreme as something I'd longed to sing ever since I began study-ing music. It presented no major technical challenges but required a stunning, faultless, fully mastered interpretation. My voice professor, an adorable bottle blonde, hadn't discouraged me from my choice. Grief would pay.

Of course, that's not the way Lucille put it; she was tactful. "Our sorrow can become our strength, Tessa."

Except when it breaks you.

Except when you hyperventilate and spend nights on the Internet waiting for pages to load with their terrifying explanations for the symptoms you're suffering from. And when the answers glue you to the couch, your hand on the remote, sorrow pushes you to gorge on American soap operas for months on end. Your sorrow has you smoking like a chimney and ruining your voice. It cripples you with cowardice and terror. And when I say *you,* I hope you understand *me.*

I only ever sang "Dido's Lament" in rehearsal.

"THE GOOD THING," Sophie said philosophically when I told her I was leaving the music faculty three months before earning my degree, "is you'll never be the girl who failed. You'll always be the bum who dropped out of university. It's better to be the dumper than the dumpee, everyone knows that."

I SPENT YEARS DAZZLED by the series of coincidences that led to my meeting Francis. One June day in 1999, a few weeks after I'd received my acceptance letter from the Université de Montréal, Sophie convinced me to come along for a two-day work stint on an eco-friendly building project. We were to lend a hand to a team of architecture grads from the University of Ottawa. It gave her an excuse to see Sean, a student she'd started dating not long before; for me, it would be an opportunity to get away and quit practising five hours a day. *You've been accepted, dummy!* Sophie, about to start in communications at UQAM, deemed that *a life well-lived* was a creator's best possible raw material.

My dad loaned us his car; I liked to drive. Sophie had found a room where we could crash (in an apartment Sean shared with a biochemistry student from Kitchener) and brought along enough CDs to take us all the way to Chicago. At the age of twenty, already deeply nostalgic, we'd been playing the same songs over and over for too long. An excessive indulgence in our favourites—Bob Dylan, Portishead, the Beatles, especially *The White Album*, *The White Album* till it was worn thin, the Police, Leonard Cohen, Carole King at Carnegie Hall, the soundtrack to *Time of the Gypsies*— was nothing short of a way of life.

Smoking with the windows down (my dad wouldn't mind, his new girlfriend Ghislaine was a smoker too), belting out renditions of "Rocky Raccoon" and "Famous Blue Raincoat," describing our plans for the future: me fleeing to Ireland because I adored the rain; the two of us escaping to Louisiana so that Sophie could track down the mysterious uncle her mother had always talked about who, according to legend, trafficked in crocodile skins ("Then I'll write an article on him and win a Pulitzer," raved Sophie); me singing an operatic version of the great TV hits of our childhood, *Rémi*, *Candy*, *Tom Sawyer*, *Care Bears*, and selling thousands of records; the two of us setting up a table on the roof of Sophie's building and, for my twenty-first birthday, inviting twenty-one people over for dinner; learning to sew, whip up cocktails, ski, make French braids.

Upon arriving in Ottawa, it quickly became clear that my "bedroom" was nothing more than a small couch in Sean's kitchen between the water heater and the sunroom. Aaron, the biochemist from Kitchener, a tall boy whose scrawniness was only matched by his pallor, offered — with little enthusiasm and not the slightest desire — to share his bed with me. I gave a nervous laugh, said I adored kitchen couches and that, at any rate, I'd be up and about before anyone else.

Sean was easygoing, amused, his hands travelling continually between his pants pockets and the wavy hair that he twirled around his finger as he spoke. He knew his charm but adored Sophie, so I abstained from commenting on the size of his ego. I let him laugh at his own jokes because they were funny and because he looked like an eight-year-old. Sean was one of those people who can bring together thirty others on a Saturday in June to scrape off paint, remove nails from planks, and fill holes in metal panels. Sophie could have done better, but she could have had worse; she already *had* had worse. Sean would do for now.

As soon as I arrived onsite, I was assigned to the snack station with three other girls. A simple task, almost absurdly so. Who couldn't help themselves to lemonade or put milk in their coffee? I kept busy sorting bags of chips by flavour. Shortly before eleven, a cry rang out to my right; a student had just jammed a rusty nail into his hand. He kept hollering — overreacting, in my view — and saying he hadn't had a tetanus shot. A girl took him to the university's nursing office, leaving the de-nailing station vacant. Bored by my conversation with the snack bar girls, I told Sean I'd take over.

My job consisted of sorting through the planks of wood and making sure that every last nail had been removed before they were reused for the house's interior finish. Once the boards had been cleaned, I delivered them to the sanders, who removed the last traces of dirt and paint flakes using rotary sanders like the one my dad had for his odd jobs: small and far from efficient. A lot of work was underway without much progress being made. Three Franco-Ontarian guys boasted about their ineptitude without a trace of pride. "I should be done by Canada Day." They laughed and guzzled Sprite. They offered me some, I took a sip, amused and a bit less shy. None of the boys interested me, and none were interested in me. Everything casual and not unpleasant.

"Okay, guys. Frank's coming with his big sander."

One of the three, Kevin, gave his fingers a snap and smiled at me, "Guess we can't be slackers forever."

Like them, I turned to see the Frank in question. He wore an ordinary T-shirt, an ugly thing depicting the effigy for the university's civil engineering faculty — a mauve maggot or was it a lightning bolt? At any rate, the thing cried "Eureka!" in a speech bubble and wore a hat reading *Class of 1994*. His outfit was rounded out with a pair of shorts, the same shorts everyone had on that summer, including me: beige workman's shorts with eighteen specialized pockets, the kind favoured by archeologists or BBC cameramen. He had thick hair; I remember thinking, *It almost looks like horsehair, there must be some pretty funny pictures of him as a kid,* and a faraway gaze—could it come from how deeply set his eyes were in their sockets? Around his neck he wore ugly mirrored sunglasses attached to a nylon cord, the beginnings of a sunburn shone on each ear, and his solid calves were impressive. *He must bike or ski or both.* The man (at least thirty) with his ugly glasses, horse's hair, and sports physique laid down his sander, smiled, and held out his hand, "Hi, I'm Francis." How to explain my shortness of breath, the Franco-Ontarians fading away, evaporating into thin air so that nothing remained in my field of vision but him and his face, my body shedding its organs, leaving nothing but a draught, an empty space, flat open country? And the only thought that crossed my mind as I stood facing this man in his hideous T-shirt—was that a coffee stain at the neck?—his forehead beaded with sweat, was, *I will never love anyone the way I love you.*

So basically, a series of coincidences. Sophie met Sean one March evening at the Mad Hatter where we went only when our McGill friends took us there, and even then, only after a lot of convincing. Sean wanted to celebrate his master's in a big way by building an eco-friendly house (actually, I found out that it was Aaron of Kitchener's idea; how could I not be fascinated by the fact that even Aaron of Kitchener had had a role in bringing Francis and me together?). Francis, a lecturer at the time and so their professor, turned up at the worksite. He saw me. It happened.

From the moment I agreed to be part of Sean's project, my encounter with Francis became a likelihood. He could have shown up at the snack bar when I was working there, or attended the end-of-project party the following night; he did, in fact. That's the night we made out like teenagers.

After borrowing Sean's old 1992 Saab—his mother's, actually—we drove into town on the pretext that the store of vodka was getting low. An hour later, with the bottle of vodka sitting on the back seat, the tangle of our bodies lay in the front between the gear shift and the tape recorder sputtering Cowboy Junkies. We had already reached that stage the day after we met. The day before, we'd shaken hands in front of the sander, traded polite jokes around a beer and had an exchange I deemed prophetic. Francis liked Leonard Cohen as much as I did. At my lowest point after our breakup, Sophie kept saying, "Who doesn't like Leonard Cohen, Tessa? Seriously, who?" But with him, I had the distinct feeling that there was a difference; this was for real. Had he known right away too? Did he show up at the wrap-up party because he knew he'd find me there? Would he have gone anyway? And if he hadn't spoken to me that first day, would he have even noticed me? Were the two of us simply destined to meet, or was it more like we were *condemned* to meet?

When Philémon was four days old, we said to ourselves, *Time for a walk*. It seemed the thing to do after two days in hospital and two days spent staring at the baby in his basket on the coffee table in the living room, asking ourselves, *What is this thing that's neither a cat nor an idea?* So Jim valiantly carried the brand-spanking-new stroller down the stairs out onto the sidewalk, then returned for the car seat—a saleswoman with a lemon-sucking smile had informed us that the seat in our stroller was too wide with too many gaps; the bucket seat, according to her, complied with prevailing regulations and was *far safer*. Jim set the car seat in the stroller using the "indispensable" plastic adapter we'd paid so dearly for, then helped me carry the baby downstairs, holding my elbow as though I were some old lady at risk of breaking a bone or two. We swaddled Philémon in all kinds of blankets, despite the summer heat, making sure to pack the baby carrier, the diaper bag, and a change of clothes as well. Our exotic destination, the drugstore, was a dozen blocks away.

The walls of our neighbourhood were made of brick and concrete and streaked with urine, and the potholed streets we ventured down, riddled with puddles dirtied by passing cars, stank of garbage cans. Where did this assault on our senses come from? Had the source always been there? It suddenly seemed indecent to deliver such a small, easily broken being into this world.

The drugstore cashier spoke too loudly. On the sidewalk, passersby tripped over the stroller; three of them just about fell on Philémon. The suvs' exhaust pipes were right at his level. And why was the sun beating down on us? Where were the tall noble trees to arch over us and provide protection as we passed?

I had spent the last few years convincing myself that the universe was an inhospitable place, but never had I felt it so brutally as that July afternoon when Philémon, Jim, and I covered the ten blocks between our apartment and the neighbourhood drugstore. What had I been thinking to impose the suffering of this existence on another being? What had gotten into me?

I PASSED THROUGH OTTAWA again with my father, three months after meeting Francis, on the way to my grandparents' cottage in Wakefield. The joyless city that is Ottawa suddenly seemed to come alive, enhanced by our romance, bathed in the golden light of my recollection of those days.

We had bought wine on King Edward Avenue. We walked along the banks of the canal to sober up from our first night together. From the phone booth in a corner of the ByWard Market, I called Sophie to tell her everything. I couldn't wait to be back at Sean's apartment and, over the phone, I did a good job conveying how lost, drunk, breathless, sated, and hooked a lover I was.

"I get what you see in him. People say he's a genius."

"Who says that? Does Sean know him well?"

"Not that well. He says he's a lit prof in an engineer's body."

"That's exactly it! A rotten description though."

"Uh-huh."

"Do you think I'm nuts?"

"I think it's the first time I've seen you respond so strongly to a human being who isn't a fictional character in a nineteenth-century novel."

"But Heathcliff, you've got to admit..."

"I do, but guess what beats an imaginary torrid affair with a dark gloomy orphan from Yorkshire? A real-life torrid affair with an engineer from the U of Ottawa."

"Even if he wears a T-shirt sporting a sombrero-capped maggot?"

"I thought it was a tripod and level—you know, the thing surveyors set up by roadways..."

"Wearing a sombrero?"

"You've got me there. But when you're in his bed, he won't be wearing his shirt."

"So you approve?"

"I approve. But get a move on. We've got to be back in Montreal by seven—your dad needs his car."

From that moment on, we were crazy in love, at least that's what I thought; I spent every waking minute making room for Francis's face in my eyes and for his voice in my ears so he'd follow me everywhere. When university started, as I shook hands and filed away my classmates' names, *Gina, Josée, Marc-Antoine, Louis-Philippe, Maria, hello, a pleasure, hi,* Francis was there with me. He was treated to an enhanced version of myself, cheerful and kind, interested and attractive in an umbrella-print skirt. His presence gave me the strength I needed no matter where I was. Often I thought, *This is love*. Both in his absence and his presence, I found much-needed strength. What did I care if he only came to see me every ten days and if he alone could call me — not that it was a stated rule, but he never asked me to call him, and since he'd just landed a promising and demanding position in a big Montreal office, I soon decided it was better to let him contact me. That way there'd be no possible doubt about his desire to speak to me. I never met his friends, except a few vague acquaintances I crossed paths with at the worksite. His family lived in a remote location (Sept-Îles, a place I knew nothing about, but immediately started reading up on) and I didn't expect him to introduce me to them this soon. I wasn't that kind of girl. Not clingy. In fact, he hadn't met my parents either. I didn't even mention him to them. Except to Étienne, a bit.

"He's old."

"You falling for some sugar daddy? Who's rocking his mid-life crisis?"

"Stop it! He's only thirty."

"He's not old. Just not as young."

"Exactly."

"Is he good to you? Does he love you?"

"He's *super* good to me."

"Does he love you?"

"It's not like I'm going to ask. And make him want to hightail it out."

"You're right. It's not the kind of thing you ask someone. But usually you can tell."

"Really?"

"So, does he love you?"

"I don't know, Étienne. I don't even know if I love him."

"I know."

"Stop it."

"No, seriously. Don't go thinking no one can tell your feet have trouble staying on the ground and that there's a Motown tune playing in your head non-stop. You're not hiding anything, sweets."

As my father's car made its way through Ottawa to hook up with Highway 105, it was true, I was almost floating. Étienne would have noticed, but he hadn't come with us that time. Ever since we were kids, we always spent each Labour Day long weekend at the cottage, all the cousins piled into the living room on makeshift mattresses because the bedrooms had already been claimed by our uncles and aunts, not to mention my dad, his girlfriend of the moment, and my grandparents, then just my grandfather when my grandmother never woke up one morning after eighty-four years of faithful service.

Étienne had a new girlfriend, a former high-school friend called Fabiola who smelled of cinnamon and tobacco. As for me, Francis had dropped by to see me a few days earlier (five to be exact; that Sunday evening he knocked at my door carrying a dozen bagels and a John Huston DVD, undressed me on the living room couch and didn't stay over, *I've got a big week ahead of me*). Based on past experience, he probably wouldn't call before Monday or Tuesday. Even if he called earlier, I loved the thought that I wouldn't be in, that he'd miss me and would suffer and wait. I knew I'd call my answering machine several times a day, telling the others I was expecting news of a job to help pay for my studies. The rare times I heard his voice on the answering machine, I imploded with joy. *Right, hello, hi, it's Francis, just calling to see what you're up to, how you're doing, call back if it's convenient, talk to you soon, ciao.* He had a funny tendency to speak in officialese. *If it's convenient.* As though I were his union rep or an insurance broker. I blamed it on his job, his education or his shyness. But I didn't let anyone else hear his messages, not even Sophie. She wouldn't have made a big deal of it because that's her nature, but I'd detect her puzzled amusement all the same. And no one was to make fun of Francis in my presence.

So I said nothing about Francis to my dad either; instead we tuned into the oldies radio stations to hear the songs we liked: Lesley Gore, Fats Domino, The Chordettes, The Shirelles, Bobby Lewis. *I couldn't sleep at all last night, just a-thinkin' of you, baby, things weren't right, well I was tossin' and turnin', turnin' and tossin', tossin' and turnin' all night.* The first person to name the singer won. We stopped in at our usual *poutinerie* just outside Wakefield. My father broke our silence once or twice to tell me stories of his childhood, stories I'd heard many times before but no matter. The repetition of words, songs, landscapes, this highway that I knew by heart, were what I wished for Francis and me.

A YEAR LATER, WE'D take to the road again, Étienne's ashes in a small plain oak urn on the back seat next to me, my father at the steering wheel, my mother in the passenger seat. Together we formed a family that had never existed. It was so grim I felt the urge to laugh. *For us to go on a family drive together, one of us had to die! Ba-dum-chssh.* Francis would laugh, wouldn't he? But Francis was gone too. Did he even know what had happened? If I called him from the same booth I'd used to call Sophie in a tizzy, would he know just from the sound of my voice that I was drowning at sea and needed him to come to my rescue?

But there was no longer anyone at the other end of the line. Francis left as he came. Before he left, we spent a summer of anticipation and rendezvous, and I don't know which of the two I loved more.

That summer, Francis was about to make the big

move from Ottawa to Montreal and we'd see each other after he'd just visited an apartment, or just before he was off to see another one. *I can come along if you want. I know my city, I'll help.* Francis turned me down gently, indicating I must have other things to do. I didn't insist. I never asked to see the one-bedroom in Rosemont he eventually chose. I'd been told that men were turned off by women who insist.

The fact that books, songs, movies, scenery, and people encountered became the fodder I used in our conversations did nothing to alter the coming disaster. In his eyes he was just seeing a girl from Montreal; in mine I was living a great love affair, exquisite and electric. I was hooked almost from the start, never complaining about his absences or the long stretches between visits. Oh, in my head, it was a whole other story. We'd feather our nest in my little apartment. I'd switch the red polka-dot shower curtain to one sporting a world map (less feminine) so we could point out countries to visit one day as we showered together. If we had friends over for dinner, I'd let him prepare something complicated and only slightly ruined, push back the furniture to add an extra leaf to the table or borrow chairs from the neighbour; sometimes he'd cup my breast with his hand as I chilled the wine, whipped the cream for the shortcake. Our sheets would be blue and smell like lime blossoms.

He broke up with me on a Tuesday in November, five months after we met, in a conversation that lasted barely ten minutes. I thought, *We never showered together.*

"I bought myself a beer-making kit."

"Really?"

"Clichéd, isn't it, an engineer who loves beer so much he wants to make it himself?"

"Real beer, with hops and all the rest?"

"With hops and all the rest."

"Even malt?"

"Yes, malt and hops, I'll have you know."

"Where do you find the malt and hops?"

"They come with the kit."

"Great!"

"You can add bark to make it more select."

"So that's what you did this week."

"That's what I did this week. Oh, and Audrey came back."

"Who?"

"Audrey, back from her year-long placement in Vancouver. Audrey, my girlfriend. I told you about her."

"I don't think so."

"I'm almost sure I told you about her."

"I'm totally sure you didn't."

"Are you upset?"

"I. Am. Surprised."

"Oh. I thought you were a free agent."

Remind yourself of all his lame sayings, remind yourself you want nothing to do with a man who uses a term like "free agent" to describe us and cover up his own cowardice.

"Uh-huh, not entirely false."

"Okay. At any rate, it was a real pleasure hanging out with you, Tessa."

Hanging out with you, hanging out with you, remember the hollow sound of those words as you roll around on the floor leaving a trail of tears in your wake.

"Okay. Great. I have to. I have to hang up now. I've got friends waiting."

"Take care, Tessa."

I didn't cry. I let myself slide down the wall to the floor, the phone between my knees. I tallied our nights and meals together. The dinner I'd prepared for him, spaghetti alla puttanesca. The time we picked up fries just fifteen minutes before midnight. The time he first walked into my bedroom, our awkward, exalted coupling. "You're built like a super chick." His civil servant speak by day, his B-movie speak by night. Looking back, it was a wonder I'd been hit as hard as I was. And yet.

Once the tears started to flow, they didn't stop for two whole days. A weekend of swollen eyes and headaches. During a moment's respite on the Saturday afternoon, I made a chocolate cake from a cake mix, with store-bought frosting. I made it round with two layers and rainbow sprinkles. It was magnificent. I stared at the cake on its pretty flowered platter—a brand new find from a flea market. As I paid, I'd promised myself that I'd use it when Francis came over. I could already see our used napkins on the table, abandoned before the meal was done, the two of us in such a hurry to get naked. The thought had been with me for weeks. Now, faced with my cake of solitude, all thought had deserted me.

THE DECISION WAS MADE that the family plot in the Amos cemetery would be the best last resting place for my brother, even though Étienne hadn't set foot in Abitibi since the age of eight and, if he could have had his say, he would probably rather have had his ashes scattered over the Grand Canyon or in the Pacific Ocean near San Francisco. A huge three-day rave at Rowardennan where his ashes could have been added to a blazing bonfire burning night and day would have suited him even better. But we weren't Étienne. We were the grief-stricken, and the euphoria created by the outpouring of love for him subsided and was followed by the undertow and total exhaustion.

Surrounded by chain-link fences and stripped of all trees (room had to be made for the tombs), the Amos cemetery evoked neither contemplation nor the dearly departed. The sun beat down mercilessly, matching our mood. But Paule liked to be home again, to see the lakes of her childhood and immerse herself in the stories of her region. In grief, my mother had left punk-dom behind.

JIM SCORED THE JOB with the orchestra the day Philémon lifted his head for the first time. I had laid him down on the change table and, as usual, I tickled his pink little belly, sang the made-up song about fish and stars and kissed the tip of his nose. Then it happened. Philémon stretched his neck out and up for the space of four, maybe five seconds. His brow furrowed, his fists clenched; this was an important milestone. I showered him with kisses, surprised at how excited I was. Babies just didn't do this at five weeks old, not unless they were extra strong! I ran to find Jim in the kitchen, "Something extraordinary's just happened." But Jim was on the phone — had it rung? since Philémon's arrival, I never heard it anymore — and he raised a finger, gently as only he knows how, to shush me. Philémon sucked patiently on my shoulder. Jim nodded. "Really happy." "Thank you, thank you so much, thank you."

When he hung up, he turned to me with a smile so filled with hope that I felt sick in spite of myself.

"I got it. I got the orchestra job."

"Really?"

"The full deal, permanent second trombone and all the benefits."

"Jim!"

"We won't be millionaires, babe, but we'll be okay. You can take all the time off you want."

"You don't know me well if you think that. I'm not going to live off you."

"I know. What I mean is you can take all the time you want with Philémon or for other projects, you can go back to school, finish your bachelor's."

"It doesn't work that way, you know."

"Maybe not."

"Well then, why suggest it?"

"I just wanted you to know. That you can do whatever you like."

"I'm not going back to singing."

"Fine."

"Does that bug you? I'm just saying, if that's what you're expecting, you're going to be disappointed. I'll never go back to singing."

"I'm not expecting anything."

Jim placed a hand on Philémon and drew me to him. If someone had seen us through the kitchen window, they couldn't have known how stiff my body was and how silent my tears.

"I'm really proud. I want you to know that. I'm so, so proud."

"I know. Me too."

"Pfft."

"Pfft yourself."

I let my head nestle on Jim's shoulder and I closed my eyes. He smelled like corn and fresh-cut grass, and his neck curved just like Philémon's.

"We'll throw you a party. We'll call our friends, drink champagne."

I thought of all our friends trooping in and catching us up on everyone's doings before taking a seat in the living room and talking loudly. Eventually, they'd agree to go out on the balcony to smoke, and the party would migrate outside. Why not stay outside? August wasn't over yet after all. They'd pass Philémon from one to the other, marvelling at the strange miracle of his presence but relieved when their turn was up. They'd start making a meal without being asked—pasta, nothing complicated, just a pot of carbonara to soak up the Spanish wine. They'd keep a running commentary going on each other's accomplishments: one girl had won a competition, another was off to Toronto, yet another was thinking of starting a quartet. From behind the bedroom door where I'd be feeding Philémon, I'd listen to them trot out anecdotes from our school days. From there I could listen without having to nod and smile, my only interest being in the silence punctuated by the sound of Philémon nursing. Nothing they could offer me — wine, jokes, energy — could make me stay with them. I was taken, promised, wonderfully walled off. I could dodge their suspicion in the face of my absent gaze, their concern, their alarmed murmuring: *Is Tessa really going to spend her life working in a bookstore and having babies? Has she actually dropped everything else for good? You won't let her do that, will you?* I thought of the friends I'd sung with, shared meals with, drunk and smoked with, demonstrated with, danced with — Alexandra, Dominic, Julie, Anne, Sunny. Their good spirits and form-hugging clothes were foreign to me now.

When I took back my offer, I didn't straighten up. Jim's shoulder felt too good.

"Actually, no friends. Just us."

Jim nodded, I wavered for a moment, then let it go. All was well.

AND YET, THERE WAS a time when I did belong to that world. Like my friends, I too had anxiously paced the halls of the music department waiting for each evaluation.

I WAS FINISHING the first semester of my third year, without brio, getting by in my classes to the best of my ability. It took a considerable amount of energy for me to behave like a normal human being in public. Wear appropriate clothing, wash my hair, make my way from point A to point B, eat soup, read a book. I sang, I took lessons, I practised. I tried to conform to what was expected of me. Back at the apartment at night, I dropped my shoes and collapsed onto the bed at last. There I was free.

A crack snaked across my bedroom wall, from the ceiling to the window trim, a broken diagonal line. I liked to think of it as an escape route for ants and spiders, imagining a passageway between the upper floor and the great outdoors, a miniature freedom walk. My eyes followed it slowly, carefully, all the way outside where the maple leaves nearly touched my window. I traced their steps, from the leaves to the branches to the trunk to the roots. The ritual soothed me. Then, unconsciously, my eyes turned back to the place where the crack began in the ceiling. I could spend hours there, interrupted only by hunger or the phone. I answered just often enough for people not to worry. I talked to my mother about my studies, the program's requirements, the rest my voice required. She was thrilled to see me studying music. "It's so wonderful that you're following your dream, Tessa. More precious than you'll ever know." I congratulated myself on being credible enough for her to believe me. Sometimes she suggested a stroll through Jeanne-Mance Park or ice cream, and my self-serving lie was clouded with guilt. Paule wanted to see me, to be a mother for more than a few minutes over the phone. She just wanted to feel relevant enough for Étienne's absence to stop its screaming.

Sometimes I'd half-heartedly agree to meet up with her or promise a movie outing, after the next evaluation or concert. At those times, her voice would swell with hope and my guilt would return; I'd pretend to have a frog in my throat or a blocked sinus and then hang up quickly, freed and ashamed. With Sophie, I didn't know how to lie; I'd steer the conversation onto other topics, to the juicy faculty gossip that she so enjoyed. Nothing of the like happened in journalism, she'd say, and the ongoing melodrama of classical music training delighted her. I could be funny and chatty then, and Sophie's laughter nourished me. She was as adept at keeping up my deceit as I was at creating it. Sometimes she'd say, "For your information, you're not fooling me." Then she'd beg me to go somewhere with her, a bar or a reception hosted by some old reporter who was her prof and who she planned to sleep with before the semester was out. Sometimes I had to say yes — there were limits to how isolated you could be or, at any rate, limits not to be breached if I didn't want to become an object of pity.

I WAS REHEARSING FOR the end-of-term recital that I harboured such great hopes for, categorically refusing to settle for less. I would sing *Beim Schlafengehen,* one of Strauss's last lieder, a superb, well-known piece that I was sure to screw up. Hadn't I gauged how thin my voice was when I tried it out in class? My soprano register, devoid of any vibrato, was really only good enough for medieval madrigals. But I stuck to my decision. I would be lyrical or nothing at all. Rehearsals, laborious and steeped in discomfort, got me nowhere. The morning of the recital, I woke up exhausted after a restless night's sleep peopled with dreams of Francis and Étienne, my departed, my despair, swimming together in a summer's lake, shouting, *Great water for the dead! Come give it a try!* I stuck to the shore, yelling at Francis that he wasn't even dead yet and that there was no worse half-assed excuse, decamping from life just to get away from a girl, goddamn coward, but no words left my lips, my head felt woolly and my eyelids heavy and, when I next opened my eyes, I realized that Étienne had disappeared beneath the water, I had spent so long focused on Francis that Étienne had slipped away once again. When I awoke, the pain was so sharp my first thought was, *Someone's cut off my arm.* I was wracked by sobs, thirty-five minutes of bawling, then the alarm clock brought me back to my senses. I would be lyrical or nothing at all. The command followed me into the washroom where I sought refuge a few minutes before my turn came up, perspiring profusely despite the snow outside, convinced I was making the worst mistake of my life and that this last humiliation in the series I'd endured since I dared to show any ambition would be the one to finally do me in. I stumbled in the hall outside the washroom, my legs gave way, they knew what was coming, I was too big a coward to make my escape, then a pair of arms caught me in extremis before I hit the floor. Arms hugged me tight, *You are here, you are alive, you are here,* and, in surrendering, all I could say was that I needed to get outside, it was a matter of life or death, and the arms acquiesced, *Yes, out we go, I'm here with you.* At one point, I managed to look up at the face speaking those words, squinting the way one does to distinguish between sea and sky, *You're in the master's program, you play trombone.* "My name's

Jim, keep going, Tessa," and when the cold December air bit into me as we stepped outside, I was surprised to hear that Jim knew my name.

In a flash of lucidity, I understood I would not be lyrical. But then, what would I be?

ONE NIGHT, MY MOTHER came to pick up Philémon and me, and we went for a drive to lull him to sleep. Summer had given way to fall, and at night the ground froze over. Concerts kept Jim out of town in Quebec City; it was the first time he hadn't been home since Philémon's birth. I adapted with delight. One day followed another, each deliciously repetitive, on top of which, I was so *busy*. I had to feed Philémon, rock him to sleep, change him, take him out for fresh air, feed him again, bathe him, and rock him to sleep. We needed no words and our silence was a thread uniting us.

On the third day, Philémon refused to sleep and his cries rang out in the apartment for two whole hours. We'd soon discovered that long car rides, preferably down an open road, were extremely effective. The ribbon of asphalt, the predictable pace, the familiar lights, and our confinement all served to calm both me and him. But Jim had taken the car, and the fierce resolve I'd exhibited in caring for Philémon alone (Wasn't my role paramount, supplanting all other issues?) suddenly weakened. I called my mother.

She arrived twenty minutes later. Philémon wailed as we put him in his car seat. His cries morphed into hiccups of despair. His forehead had turned a purplish red, except for an orb of flesh about the size of a nickel that stayed white even in the throes of anger, as though the spot had been blessed.

We took the road up the mountain where it was easier to drive without having to stop for traffic lights. In twenty minutes, it would be midnight. Philémon stopped crying almost immediately. "Do you want to go home?" my mother asked. "You must be exhausted." She seemed wide awake, as though her day had just begun. I was rocked by the car's motion, and a lilting rain sprinkled the windows. "Better to wait a bit longer, let him drift off for good." Philémon was sound asleep; I knew his slightest breath by heart and the slow, low rumbling, surprising coming from such a small resonance chamber, didn't lie. But Paule's hands guided the steering wheel with, yes, that's what it was, hope, and the rain falling over the city, the Mount Royal cemetery appearing through the window, gave permission to be both accompanied and silent. "Let's drive a bit longer." She radiated joy. I settled back in my seat, laid my head against the headrest and closed my eyes. Where was Francis tonight? What was he doing? At the top of the mountain sat a girl whose bed he'd shared five years earlier, a girl no longer a girl but a mother, her shredded heart slowly beginning to beat again for a man other than him, and she was grateful. Did he know she was loved?

Would it have changed anything?

WITH THE FIRST SNOWFALL came shorter afternoons. Philémon's life took on the shape of the ordinary. Night was night, day was day, and his presence felt like a foreign city where you'd lived just long enough to know where to go to buy bread. Sophie, who I'd met up with on Laurier for an omelette and a walk with Philémon, was planning a trip to Thailand and quickly reassured me that Nathan, whom she'd just met and with whom she meant to travel, was reliable. This ritual dated back to the days when Sophie would head out on a whim, either by bus or hitchhiking, for adventure-filled weekends, sometimes with a guy she was interested in, sometimes with a girlfriend more game than me, and she would ask me to cover for her with her parents. She'd tell them she was invited over to a friend's cottage (usually Élise's or Marie-Joëlle's, or Jeanne's, whose hippyish parents never called other parents to inquire about their offspring), careful to point out that, given the rustic location, there'd be no phone or electricity. I was the only one who knew that she was actually headed to the bus terminal where she'd pick a destination at random. (*Kingston, Ontario. Kingston, like in Bob Marley's songs! Let me tell you, Tessa, it was no Jamaica*). I made her promise to call every day, tell me where she was sleeping and with whom. If she didn't come back as planned, it was up to me to fly to her rescue. As a bonus, I liked the bravado I felt by proxy without having to leave the comfort of Mozart's *Requiem* score that I had to learn for the next concert.

Now that we were grown, Sophie no longer had to lie to her parents. But the habit remained.

"Didn't Nathan give you shit the other night for not calling when you were supposed to call?"

"Everyone gives me shit for that."

"Not me."

"But you're my friend."

"Shouldn't the guy you're sleeping with be your friend too?"

"Okay. It may not be ideal."

"You have no business flying to the other side of the world with someone who's going to blow a fuse whenever you show an interest in something other than him."

"He's not like that."

"He's a little like that. Write in code if you think he's reading your emails."

"I should have met up with you closer to your place. It'll take you an hour to walk home pushing that stroller."

"It puts the baby to sleep, no worries. I could make a career out of it. Baby walker. There must be a market, mustn't there?"

"You can make a career out of whatever you want, my friend."

"Shut up."

"Back at you."

Evening was upon us and it felt good to be sur-rounded by men rushing home from work and women shivering in high heels. At this time of day, any other strollers I saw were returning from daycare. Tired-looking mothers shoved half-croissants into their screaming toddlers' pudgy fingers to take the edge off their hunger or maybe just to shut them up. I knew that my pace and the absence of a briefcase gave me away. *That one's still on maternity leave.* They didn't know that I'd dropped out of university just three months before my degree to sell books on Côte-des-Neiges for two years before I got pregnant and that my leave was, in fact, dragging on. I wondered what would happen if I decided to stay on maternity leave forever, whether the stroller would become a scooter, then a bicycle, and whether the woman the windows reflected back at me would always walk at the same leisurely pace. Who would care?

It was the blessed hour when lights go on in houses and curtains have not yet been drawn. I could walk the streets around our house — the nap could last a bit longer, I didn't want to go home yet, Jim would be at rehearsals until late this evening — and spy on other people's lives. Here a living room with an old kitschy chandelier and one whole wall made of bookcases. There a motley arrangement of two beds squeezed into a child's tiny bedroom. A bright ceiling light, dimmerless, illuminating a set of sofas in burnt orange velvet. And TVs. Lots of TVs, a chain of blue-tinted, flickering living rooms facing screens broadcasting the news or a game show. Private disasters and empty shells, mired in conformity. Taking the alley to the back door, my eyes met those of a young teen. She couldn't have been more than fifteen, and her eyes gazed outward just as mine had shifted inward. I thought, *I know them all.*

At that moment, there was nothing more I needed.

Lenny

"Are we still on for tomorrow?"

"Tomorrow."

"You're going to a party, no?"

"Oh. Yes. A party. Charles's fortieth."

"When would you like me to be there?"

"Tomorrow, Charles's fortieth."

"What?"

"Saturday, tomorrow."

"Could you quit mumbling? You know how hard of hearing your old mother is."

"Yes, uh. Yes. Let's say six. Six o'clock, how does that sound? You could come earlier too."

"If I come earlier, I could look after dinner."

"That's not your job, you know."

"Look, I don't mind making supper for my grandsons. I can make them fries, they like fries."

"That's true."

"But if you'd rather have me come later..."

"No. Let's say five. Let me."

"Is your deep fryer still broken?"

"It wasn't broken. It was just dirty."

"No need to bring mine then?"

"No, no need."

"Do you have any canola oil?"

"I don't know. I think it's gone bad."

"You think everything's gone bad."

"That's not true."

"I'll bring mine. I just bought it. It hasn't gone bad."

"I believe you."

"You can smell it if you like."

"I said I believe you."

"I'll make them some fish too. They don't eat enough fish."

"I make fish at least once a week."

"Not enough white fish. You only make salmon."

"Let me get back to you to confirm."

"What?"

"I'll confirm it with you on Saturday morning. Jim's been getting migraines lately. He might cancel."

"I could come anyway. Especially if he's getting migraines. That way he can rest."

"We'll see. We'll see."

"You sound strange. Are you talking and driving at the same time?"

"Yes."

"I'm hanging up."

"I'm hands free, Mom."

"I'm still going to hang up. Was there anything else you wanted to tell me?"

For a fraction of a second, I think of telling her everything. *Mom, I'm going to see my old boyfriend, no, boyfriend may be too strong a word, more like a glorified lover. I'm to meet him out in front of Lenny's at half past twelve, then I'll follow him downtown, most likely to a hotel room, at first I thought we'd do it in the car, but then I remembered we're grown-ups now, he'll soon be forty-five. Forty-five-year-olds don't get it on in cars, they pay for a hotel room and wash their hands after peeing, so I'll follow him to a hotel room, like the love that's followed me and inhabited me and defined me for so long—yes, Mom, it defined me, even though I never told you about him and you don't know either his name or his face, but you can't hold it against me, did you tell that kind of stuff to your mother? No, just what I thought, it's much too fragile and precious to be brought up between the main course and dessert, but believe you me, being possessed this way, I may very well never come back from this love affair. I'll throw myself headlong beneath those sheets with him, only to emerge weeks later or perhaps never, because why leave the bed of a man you've spent so long waiting for? Not to take people out to visit a few houses, right, Mom? In other words, you won't be babysitting this Saturday because I won't be there anymore and Jim won't feel like going out, although, come to think of it, he might need to go on a bender, screw the first woman he meets, down one shooter after another, who knows, you'll probably babysit the kids after all, just let me get back and confirm.*

"No, that's all."

"Okay. Have a good day then."

"You too."

Have a good day—those were my words to Philémon and Boris this morning as I watched them step onto the school bus. Boris has soccer today; he was thrilled. He loves to swim, run, climb. He won't need me much longer. I could see the boys' profiles backlit by the sun; they'd found their seats on the bus and exchanged manly handshakes with their friends. I gave a discreet wave. For the last time *before*.

It's a glorious day out, a day for snow to melt, for leather and leafbuds, a day for undressing with the window wide open. Oscar whistled as he trotted to daycare, his neck curved just like Jim's, *my three boys are carbon copies of their father*, and he giggled at the sight of his friends—Édouard, Milos, Nana, the ones he sees every day, yet his joy never wavers; he has also inherited Jim's unfailing love. *Have a good day*, I told Jim, he kissed me again, a long, insistent kiss, and if I hadn't already known that he lavishes affection as freely as newspapers are handed out at subway entrances, I would have thought, *He knows.*

Everything's normal, I keep telling myself. *Everything's normal, but soon it won't be.*

GUYLAINE IS HAPPY. SHE can't figure out why I'm offering her a listing on a silver platter.

"Oh my God, West Ahuntsic, that's magic, houses are kept up around there, they bring in great clients, people who know the real value of things 'cause there's all kinds of rich people who buy McManors across the river, but West Ahuntsic is somethin' else again, it's people with taste who look to live there. D'you mind if I fiddle with the listing description?"

I told Guylaine that I was getting rid of certain listings because I wanted a relaxing summer, my last one before my eldest heads off to secondary school, and we wanted to go on tour with Jim. Guylaine believed me. She has a twenty-two-year-old daughter and they're super close (regular trips to the spa, clothes swapping, and double-dates with their boyfriends). My feeling is that she's found a friend in her daughter more than anything else. My tribe both alarms her and elicits her admiration. She makes a big deal about all the sacrifices I've made. *Oh! You're such a good mom, Tessa*. I don't contradict her since it comes in handy when I want to skip some evening reception or pass off a compromising listing in West Ahuntsic.

I don't go into the office very often. Even though I manage to collect juicy anecdotes there for Jim about Agostino's conquests or Jacques's body odour (spaghetti sweat à la *Eau Sauvage*), the fact is that with its soundproof panels, harsh lighting, and dismally patterned carpets, the place feels like my tomb. Even though I'm a realtor, I don't need a daily reminder.

Today the office seems different. It's as though the windows, which can't be opened for love or money, have let spring air into the cubicles, and several times I ask Voula, the receptionist, if someone's changed the lighting. "No, it's just a gorgeous day." This *gorgeous day* brimming with the promise of my secret rendez-vous suddenly makes me want to buy everyone flowers. Don't they deserve something, these hardworking co-workers, with their silk ties and synthetic jackets, reasonably heeled shoes and layered haircuts? After concerts, soloists are buried in flowers. From time to time, Jim brings home a bouquet left behind by an overladen diva. But the soloists sang to hundreds of already charmed people, experienced the incomparable pleasure of hearing their voices reverberate within the confines of a rapt room, sent notes soaring on the exquisite, textured layers produced by their supporting musicians, so they had already received both the best and the most. Why offer them flowers too? Flowers are for realtors and their receptionists holed away in some franchise's wan offices, people who elicit distrust and are loved by no one really. *They have it easy, they rake in the big bucks*—that's true at times, but doesn't make the work any less burdensome.

If I have time before noon, I'll go to Beaubien to buy tulips. I'll place one bunch on Voula's desk and another in the shared kitchen. An appeasement of sorts, a consolation prize for those whose lives won't change today or tomorrow or next year. My way of telling them, *You don't have my courage, but even cowards should be entitled to things of beauty.*

It's ELEVEN THIRTY WHEN I set foot in the house again. I ruled out wearing my star-motif dress first thing in the morning. Not that Jim would have been suspicious. He'd have thought it looked beautiful or rather he'd have thought I looked beautiful, me in my dress, and said, *Oscar, look at how beautiful Mom is.* Oscar would have given a Nutella-smeared smile and wrapped his arms around my neck; no way did I want to witness that display. So I followed my usual routine: no eye makeup, no curling my hair. A morning like any other when I did what I always do, got up, got dressed, ate, got ready, and said goodbye on the landing, in front of the school bus or the daycare worker.

At half past eleven I return home — nothing unusual about that either, up to now my life is as it always has been and it doesn't faze me, just the opposite in fact. I feel something akin to amusement at how conscious the gestures have become and, turning the key in the door, think, *I'm saying my goodbyes.* I do make sure that Jim has left though. Last night, just before sinking into a fitful sleep, he told me about the next day's rehearsal and how the meeting afterwards hung over him; things could get ugly because of the announced cutbacks, he'd have to be the referee. Jim had a tough day at work ahead of him, and I urged him to get right to sleep so he'd *be at his best.* He dozed off, his hand on my thigh. I didn't give a second thought to his worries. After all, I had the end of a world to get ready for. I am the one who has set out to hijack his plane and who locked the cockpit when the co-pilot stepped out to go to the washroom; I turn off the automatic pilot and let my desire or my despair decide what's to come. I won't look back, no matter how much the innocent beg.

The star dress waits patiently in the closet. I pull on my black panties and bra, nothing exceptional — I'm not about to pretend I'm more than I am. I slip into my gold ballerina flats. I take care with my makeup, not overdoing it. The woman he knew has aged; it was only four days ago that we last saw each other, but today reunites us. I'll not touch my hair. It does what it wants anyway and I don't have enough time for the curling iron. In forty minutes, I'll be outside Lenny's with Francis, and the birds will sing the Pet Shop Boys version of "Always on My Mind" as they drape us in pink and blue spring ribbons once and for all.

Before leaving, I stop in the kitchen and open the fridge. Bread, cheese, ham, mustard, a bit of leftover rice, some chicken, half a red cabbage. Enough to make croque-monsieurs, a soup, or coleslaw with. Or they can order in, if what's here isn't to their liking. At any rate, my eclipse is only temporary—I'll return transformed, isn't that what everyone says? You have to be happy to make others happy, you have to love yourself to be loved? The children's mother will be transformed and they will say, *Thank you, Mom, for transforming yourself, we are happy.*

FRANCIS AND I NEVER really did visit Lenny's. The night we ventured over, he was out. September had the same effect as that first night in June when Francis wore a fawning look. Truth be told, he'd had more to drink than usual. We'd downed a cheap bottle of wine in a restaurant a few blocks away and felt like drinking some more once we sat down on the park bench across from Lenny's. Francis ran to the corner store, his unsteadiness tripping him up endearingly, only to return with something acidic and sweet, the kind of wine that, with one whiff, can bring on a migraine, but in those days, we drank it like water. It was a Friday, Saint-Laurent was teeming with crowds, and we enjoyed watching the cars and stores light up as the night advanced. No lights on at Lenny's though.

"Is this really it?"

"Uh-huh."

"How do you know?"

"Any self-respecting girl from Montreal knows."

"Scorn suits you."

"Paternalism suits you."

Francis laughed, then popped the rim of the bottle in my mouth to shut me up. Wine dribbled down my chin, a few drops landing on my pale blue linen dress. The next day, the dress trailing on my bedroom floor ended up on a hanger, forgotten in the closet. I only found it again months later, after we broke up, the dried wine stains looking like blood from a wound, and I cried all night long.

But back then, Francis and I sat staring at a stone house nestled between a triplex and an alley across from Parc du Portugal, and tried to guess which room went with which window.

"That must be the living room there."

"Or his bedroom."

"I'm sure his bedroom doesn't look out onto the street."

"Unless it's up top."

"Do you think his children still have theirs?"

"How old are they?"

"I don't know. Your age."

"'Your age'? The claws are out."

"Ha, ha. Watch your blood pressure, Grandpa."

"At any rate. Lenny's not one for going out."

"For years I've walked by his place as often as I could, but I've never seen him. I must have eaten eight hundred times at Bagel, Etc., hoping to cross paths with him. They say he goes to Beauty's too. But I never saw him there either, nothing. Sophie and I made it our mission."

"What would you say to him if you did see him?"

I shrugged. *That's not the point*, I thought, surprised he hadn't figured it out from the start. I didn't explain. We drained the bottle and tottered back to my apartment where we made half-hearted, spark-free love. It was hot, we were drunk.

Doubled up over my stained dress, what I remembered was a sublime, perfect evening and, at its core, the howling pain of being expelled from paradise.

TODAY THE STONE house seems smaller but straighter. On the facing bench, two men wearing grey golf caps and windbreakers chat in Portugese. A coughing spell interrupts their conversation, but they soon pick up again where they'd left off.

I shouldn't call him Lenny. Over the phone on Tuesday, the expression sounded out of place, almost embarrassing to my ears. I don't know the man, after all. And I'm past the age where I could be that brazen. As I sit on the steps to the pavilion in Portugal Park staring at the ceramic tilework, my eyes don't know where to look, *not at the street, if he comes he'll see me searching him out and it'll make me look like some crazy person, why didn't I bring something to read, why did I want to be here before him, at the time it seemed like a good idea, a way of protecting myself, giving me time to stake out my territory: come if you dare, Francis, I'm here and I'm not afraid.* It's still ten minutes before the appointed hour and I consider walking around the block, no one will know, the two old Portugese men won't say a word, what would they have to say to some matron in a dress made for summer? I tell myself to stand up, but my legs won't obey. Blame it on the chilly weather— *What were you thinking, stupid, going out without tights in April*—or the shadow of an idea that has just popped into my head, as dark as it is clear, *None of this makes any sense,* whispering that this will solve nothing, that my star-motif dress is the height of absurdity and that no one, not even Francis, and even less so Lenny, can escape the inescapable. Then there he is, in the park, shading his eyes with his hand, any second now he'll have spotted me, it's too late to leave, *but you wanted to come, you bought a dress, what were you expecting, imbecile?* and now he's approaching with the smile of the little boy he used to be, and all else vanishes— my certainties and fears, the park that's nothing but a square, the old Portugese men, the ceramic tilework, and Leonard Cohen's lovely stone house.

I'M FREEZING ALL OF a sudden. My perforated flats let
air in between my toes, and I'm still as cold even after
I button my coat and raise the collar. As for Francis, he
came in his winter clothes. He's wearing a teal padded
jacket, his look halfway between a CEO on holiday and
a comely horticulturist in uniform. He has forgotten
neither his gloves nor his scarf. *Jim always forgets his
scarf.* I realize that this failing of his fills me with pride;
I must be more twisted than I'm ready to admit. I set
my purse on my lap to create another barrier between
the wind and me.

"You could see the cold snap coming."

It's all there, the glint in his eye, the ironic lilt to
his voice: Francis teasing. But something in his words
doesn't bounce back, and I'm surprised at having to
grope for an answer.

"April showers bring May flowers."

That's all I managed to come up with. And I said it out loud. *April showers bring May flowers.* Christ. Must be nerves. It will take time and liquor for my tongue to loosen up. Meanwhile we can talk about the weather, our only glue being increasingly vague memories of a past in each other's arms.

"I wasn't sure you'd come."

"Me neither."

"But you did."

"You too."

"We both did."

"To Lenny's house."

The expression still irritates me. Even my mother would have raised an eyebrow, *Is that what the happy few call him?* And I'd pull a face, *No one says* Lenny, *Mom, but they don't say* happy few *either.*

"He isn't home, you know."

"Such is life."

Whatever happened to my gift for repartee? Where's the witty banter that, just three days ago on his door-step, welled up like water through the breach in a dike?

"Should we go for a drink?"

"Probably a good idea."

He suggests, I agree, disguising my nerves under a singsong tone. The two old Portugese men glance at us as we walk past their bench. I could flatter myself thinking they're looking at my bare legs. But I could also tell myself these are far from the first they've seen, experts as they are in lovers' trysts in Portugal Park. They can already tell that ours will end in a catastrophe. *You could tell by the way the gentleman leaned away from her,* one will say in Portugese. *More by the way the lady looped a strand of hair behind her ear, like a child fiddling to relieve her boredom,* the other will say, in Portugese as well.

I HAVEN'T COME HERE for years. I don't often go to bars anyway, but the ones I do go to tend to not let customers drop peanut shells on the floor, whereas this establishment has maintained, from day one, the right for people to do just that, while insisting on serving nothing but beer, cheap and strong. *It's a bar, what do you expect?* I don't know, but as I sit down by the window (wouldn't it have been better to sit discreetly at the back by the pool tables like the lovers we would soon be?), I'm surprised to notice that, despite the envy I'd felt catching sight of its idle clientele as I drove by on my way from one appointment to another, from daycare to school or from the liquor store to the butcher's, the bar no longer evokes the least bit of excitement. The black paint on the walls doesn't hide their age or disrepair. The scattered patrons sit hunched over, their conversations banal.

"I spent one evening here."

"Only one."

"I mean, a memorable one. Didn't I ever tell you?"

Francis has his eye out for the waiter, who has his back to us and is busy shelving bottles of beer. "Want me to order at the bar?" Francis sounds confident, almost eager, his hands already on the table ready to push him to his feet.

"He'll see us eventually." My tone is curt, like fingers snapping. I hadn't meant it to come across as a reproach, *seriously, I need a beer too*, but the echo of my brusqueness hovers briefly between us. "I want to tell my story."

I give him my winning smile, a charmer's trick I've basically never used on anyone other than Jim after a glass of bubbly. Today I refuse to be the bad guy. Francis inches forward on his chair, the furrows in his brow disappear. I've got him.

"I was sixteen but looked twenty."

I have a sudden urge to add, *Like today, I'm thirty-seven but I look forty, and not today's forty but a 1960s forty.* But that would break my enchantress spell, wouldn't it?

"You hung out in bars when you were sixteen?"

"Everyone did, Francis. That's not the interesting part."

He turns toward the bar again. The waiter still has his back to us.

"I had a crush on a guy a lot older than me."

"How old was he?"

"Twenty-four? Twenty-six?"

"You were sixteen?"

"That's not the interesting part either."

"Oh, it isn't?"

"Are you sure I never told you the story?"

"I don't think so."

A picture comes to mind. Francis and I nestled in the bed I had as a young adult. It's July, the air is thick and humid, I tell him the anecdote, laughing, he finds me adorable, and I dare add—in fact, that's probably why I remember it—I find myself adorable, *so nice to have a story to tell.*

"I met him at my father's company Christmas party. He was the waiter. All I knew about him was his name and what he was studying. When I left to get my coat on my way out, he drew me into a corner of the cloakroom and kissed me open mouthed."

"Shit, that's terrible."

"You mean wonderful. It was the kind of thrill I'd been waiting for since grade nine. I relived it for weeks afterwards. So much so that I set out to find him. I knew his university and faculty. I actually wrote to his professor, who was the department director, a very polite letter claiming that I was a distant relative of the fellow and I tucked another sealed letter into the envelope for him. I told him I wanted to see him again, even though he'd probably make fun of me, but I would regret it if I hadn't at least tried. One month later, he called!"

"He would have been crazy not to."

"He suggested we meet here, so I told my mom I had to study with Sophie at her house, and everything was set."

"Weren't you afraid he'd be some kind of maniac?"

"I was the maniac."

"What happened?"

"Kurt Cobain had just died. Sophie and I wrote an article on his death for the school paper. You remember my friend Sophie, don't you? A real tearjerker of an article, heartfelt, super awkward. I was so proud of it that I brought it with me to show him. 'Kurt Cobain wrote "I love and feel sorry for people too much," in the note he left for his wife Courtney Love. For our part, we promise to honour him by listening to his music for the rest of our lives.'"

"You showed the guy the article for your high-school paper?"

"I know. Not the best seduction ploy. All of a sudden, he felt really old and started casting nervous glances all around, panic stricken at the thought he might be arrested for statutory rape. A bit like you right now."

"Me? I'm not glancing around. Other than at the waiter who's ignoring us."

"Hmm."

"What, hmm?"

"Hmm."

"You women don't play fair. You say you're all for communication but love nothing more than a bit of mystery."

"I'll go order. You want a beer?"

You women. You women this. You women that. Walking over to the deserted bar, I try to think of a retort to the sweeping statement Francis just made. Back in the day, I'd have had no trouble countering him, stirring the pot, making him laugh with my unerring gift for repartee. The game is part of who we are. So why don't wisecracks come to me anymore? *We women thank you for your remark. We women thank you men for this remark that fosters an evolution in gender relationships. I will call* UQAM's *chair for feminist studies at once so we can hold a colloquium on the groundbreaking discovery.* Why not? Why jump up to order something at the bar instead? Could I — the very question breaks my heart — be bored?

What's weird is that I've been having conversations with Francis in my head for the past fifteen years. He was present as I resolved many an inner conflict. I had only to call on him for my rapier-like wit to don its smartest sequin-studded suit and grab the mic. I imagined his laughter at my provocative tirades and his delight in the way I virtually tore into my opponents — the crazy driver on Highway 40, the gung-ho mother on the school foundation board, former friends who continued on as artists, whose star, despite their mediocrity, stubbornly refused to fade—I spared no one and my audience loved every minute of it. Francis told me so often how he loved my twisted mind. He and I against the sorry world peopled with sheep and sellouts, blah blah, blah blah. But those versions of us no longer exist.

Isn't it blindingly clear? Can this still be my heart-throb lover? His greying and, worse yet, straggly hair—actually, not so much straggly as downy, the tragicomedy of men as they age, who end up looking like ducklings for a while, as harmless as cotton candy—his altered hair, at any rate, and then the clothes, the same kind he went in for back then, but that now give him a sad air, this flesh-and-bones Francis, in short, what has he been doing in my fantasies? Isn't he as ridiculous as me in my depressed, getting-on-in-years garb?

Is he as painfully ashamed as I am?

Aren't we just a couple of sadsack clowns in a time-worn skit?

"For your boyfriend it's full price, for you it's free."

With the light behind him, I have trouble seeing the barman at his till. Tall and thin, his delivery slow and playful. I frown. *How lame.*

"Hi, Tessa."

I shift to the left to see him in the light. Anthony. That glistening, jumpy kid from my dad's Camry has grown up — he's closing in on thirty-five — and is now a head taller than me. His smile still harbours something of a child, and he still wears a baseball cap pulled down low on his brow, but an outsider looking in would make no mistake: these two who have just recognized each other have both left their younger years behind.

"Anthony. It's been a long time."

"Our parents broke up the day I turned fourteen. Going on twenty-one years ago."

"I forgot it happened on your birthday. That's awful."

"Yes, it wasn't that classy a move on your dad's part."

"I'll say."

"He did remember to buy chips for my party. Then my mom tried to make it better by tripling the number of presents I got. It wasn't all bad."

Anthony flashes a glimpse of his teeth. He's bitter now, like us all.

"What would you like?"

"Two beers, thanks."

"I heard about your brother."

"Yes."

He pulls out two bottles of lager, Dutch or Belgian, it doesn't matter to either of us. I didn't think to ask Francis what he wanted.

"I saw your name up on a sign."

"Ha. Yes. Famous me."

"I'm happy for you."

"How are you doing?"

He tells me about his little family, pulls out his cell-phone to show me pictures—a boy a girl a woman to love, karate and ballet lessons, plans to move to the south shore, holidays up north. Anthony is happy. I tell him about my boys, the science fair, life in Villeray, Jim's orchestra, my parents who are doing well, thanks. Back at the table, Francis's phone is keeping him busy. Anthony holds the beer out to me, won't hear of me paying. I insist; so does he. Both of us know the conversation is languishing and that it's best to stop here. I take the beer.

"He's not my boyfriend."

Anthony holds my gaze an instant. I don't leave quite yet, just back up a step, a passenger steadying herself as the bus hits the brakes. Do I think he has something to teach me? That he can reveal what he saw looking at me seated at a table in my girly dress with a man who's not my husband on a Friday afternoon in the spring? Of course, Anthony hasn't seen me for twenty years—maybe he thinks I wear star dresses every day and maybe he sees what I see in the mirror: a belly-aching kid who's grown older. Maybe he's already in a hurry to get home and tell his wife, *Remember that little brat I told you about, her dad Yves is the guy my mom lived with in the nineties, that girl who spent the whole summer holiday in '93 trying to humiliate me and then bitched about my mom's presents? She turned up today in the bar dressed like a piñata and sat with a man who couldn't stop looking at his watch. Maybe there is some justice after all.*

"Let me know if you need anything."

That's all he says. No spite, no scorn in his voice, no clue that might make me think he wishes me ill, *Let me know*, that's all. He even smiles, a generous something in his pupil. *Don't lose your way*, is what he may be thinking. *Your home is north after the underpass, after Little Italy, not far from Jarry Park. Take Saint-Laurent then keep on walking all the way home in a straight line, no big deal, you think that adventure lies around here? Adventure lies with your feet. Grab your coat, leave this place, start walking, pass Mont-Royal, Laurier, Bernard, Beaubien, Dante, pass De Castelnau, it's straight ahead, Tessa.*

No, that's me thinking.

I bring the beer back to our table, give Francis his, we take a few sips, our tongues loosen somewhat, laughter rings out after all, and the game, the waltz, is okay. But that's probably because I know that, within the hour, I'll have said goodbye to Francis and started walking north. I know that for a fact, and I can hardly wait.

He polishes off his beer in next to no time. Some nervous—or violent—edge has him drinking in great gulps, never setting his bottle down. I take long swigs, as though I'd just finished the traditional July move to a new place and expected nothing more from the day. I'm going to have to tell him, and I dread that moment. The same way I'd dread calling our neighbourhood school to announce that a select institution had accepted our child's application and so he wouldn't be back to class, sorry, goodbye. A brief stab of guilt followed by near indecent euphoria. Now that's over and done with. I'm rid of the shadow that's hung over me for a week, the ghost of misfortune to come, holding out some cursed parallel universe, but Francis and I live in the same universe, in the same *city*, and my life with him would only have been a variation on the life I have led up to now, what wouldn't have changed is me, I'll never escape myself. Although that thought may weigh me down enough to grasp at dresses and sentimental recollections, it no longer crushes me as much as having sought refuge in a rundown bar on Saint-Laurent Boulevard one Friday afternoon.

Francis sets his bottle on the table just as I take my fourth swig.

"Another round?"

His question is hurried, his eyes searching for Anthony, who's chatting with customers. I note his hands on the bottle. He has a boy's short, slender fingers, smooth skin almost free of flaws. No freckles, no hair, no red patches from work or the weather. His hands fascinate me, hands of plaster. All of a sudden, I miss Jim and my need to see and touch him becomes acute, imperative.

A LITTLE OVER a year ago, Boris tore open his knee jumping off the diving board during a school outing. The pain was so great he passed out in the water. Someone got him out right away, but he had to be transported to the hospital and for several hours — horrific, helpless hours — the fear of losing him had us paralyzed.

Staff at the school managed to get through to Jim first. I was on an appointment, a deed of sale for an overpriced property on Gouin Boulevard. I checked my messages on my way out, and my fingers went numb the way they used to when I'd sit on my hands as a child then take them out again from under my thighs.

Jim was waiting at the hospital. I kept looking for Boris everywhere and Jim had to hold me with both hands to stop me from turning in circles. He described the accident and then sat me down on a straight-backed chair in the hallway, went for some chocolate and, when I turned to look, I saw my mother at my side, her two hands clutching her purse, like a little old lady, *My mother has shrunk.* I don't know who called her. Most likely Jim.

I couldn't bear thinking of possible scenarios. I focused on my mother's hands, their lined veins, speckles of light brown, agile, not the slightest trembling, but nevertheless clutching her leather purse by the seam where the red dye had worn away from years of handling. She'd had the purse for a long time; maybe I gave it to her one Mother's Day or birthday, Christmas, I didn't remember, but a long time ago whenever it was; the purse was well-worn. I was seized by a sudden desire to grab it, empty its contents on the floor, throw it into the garbage can. *Go buy a new purse, Mom. Your ghost purse weighs on me.* One of her hands reached over to cover mine — I'd been rubbing the fabric of my pants endlessly — and her touch made me stop. "Boris is made to last. He'll pull through."

When your mother tells you your son is made to last

and that he'll pull through, you don't argue, you nod, you believe. But I wasn't as sure that Boris was made to last. He had to be, I guess, to be the second child of such a sad woman, caught as he was in the vice between a stellar elder son and a sun-filled youngest, he had to be in order not to miss a single day of school. Of course, Boris had had the occasional cold, a wintertime fever or two, but I had never received that call from school. *Ma'am? This is the secretary here. Your son isn't feeling well. Your son threw up in the hall, the teacher thinks he's running a temperature. Your son has a nasty cough. Could you come and pick him up?* No, not Boris. Boris left his dirty clothes lying around everywhere, soaked in his young athlete's sweat. He kept his Lego blocks for months on his bedside table. He was an expert on Marvel and DC Comics. He had a voracious, insatiable appetite. *At the age of seven, he eats like a teenager. What will it be like when he's fifteen?* Secretive, an island unto himself, he would soon be eight, and it was with a feeling of absolute horror, as he lay in intensive care, that I realized I barely knew my son.

"You know him better than anyone. You know he'll pull through."

Had she heard my thoughts? Paule patted my thigh, two or three weak taps, the way you absentmindedly caress the head of a child who's been speaking for too long. *I know absolutely nothing, Mom. I've been wrong so often. I know nothing of what it takes to raise children and keep them from dying. I don't know what this life is I'm leading or why.*

Jim reappeared, holding the chocolate out to me, and hugged my mother. They spoke softly, as though I were sleeping or we were in church. Yet Sainte-Justine Hospital's PA system showed no such decency; there was no sotto voce, no lilt to the squeal of cart wheels. No beauty worthy of silence. So I too spoke, loudly, "Why can't we wait by his room?"

Jim turned to me — my outburst gave them a start — with fury in his eye, a look I'd seen before on days I'd been unfair. "Because we'd disturb them. Because they've got a job to do. I'm not going to stop them from doing their job just as they're saving my son's life."

My mother took a deep breath then held it, a habit I've seen since childhood, a sort of backwards sigh, filling up with air then never letting it out, usually to my intense irritation, imprisoning me with her aborted breath. This time I followed suit, I swallowed Jim's words and his stern short-lived tone, and just then, a physician arrived to take us to our son.

The banality of our surroundings surprised me at first. I had spent the past few hours imagining a green, windowless, ceramic-tiled room, the way operating rooms used to be, and Boris lying on a hard, cold metal table, his small bare shoulders drained of all colour by the light of a too-harsh lamp. Instead the room had the same pink walls as the maternity wing and an almost inviting-looking bed placed by a window. Boris lay beneath several blankets, his head turned to face the outdoors. The sun was setting and the room was bathed in an orange-hued light and his hair looked red (it's so short, I'd begged him to wear his hair long in all its copper splendour, but Boris hates having to brush hair off his face, since the age of five he's kept it short the way a professional athlete would). He took a slow breath, his arms buried in warmth, and blinked regularly as though following instructions.

The last time he'd been in this hospital was for Oscar's birth. He'd drawn a picture of a family on construction paper with his fruit-scented felt markers. The page was slightly ripped and Boris had scribbled our names under our likenesses: "Papa, Maman, Philémon, Boris, baby." Jim, Philémon, and I were giants; Boris was a bird on Jim's shoulder. Oscar, in the middle, was a flea whose extra-long arms surrounded us all.

The time before that had been for his own birth.

"Boris?"

He turned his head slowly, and his lips quivered. For an instant, it felt as if he didn't recognize us, as if we had become strangers to him—well-meaning ones of course, but strangers all the same. Terror stricken, I thought, *He's seen that look before, in my own eyes.* But soon enough his eyes opened wide, and the irresistible light he'd inherited from Jim shone on his face. "Mom." The word had the effect of a detonator; l leaned over to shower him with kisses, suppressing my questions, but then no, I asked if he was hungry, if he was thirsty, if he was warm enough, if he was afraid. Jim laid a hand on my shoulder and I stopped, even though his hand wasn't there to tell me to be quiet, but to hold back the tide. I closed my eyes and the air trapped in my lungs for hours finally escaped.

"I'm sorry." Boris, so tiny in his hospital bed, was apologizing. Jim's reaction was immediate: he shed tears on Boris's forehead as he swore Boris had no reason to apologize. Boris nodded but he, too, was crying, he explained he *hadn't wanted to do anything dumb.* "Mehdi and Paul said I was too chicken to jump off the third board, and maybe it was true but what do you do when you're too chicken, I thought I didn't have a choice, I banged my knee on the diving board, I don't even remember hitting the water, I'm sorry, I'm really sorry."

Jim wrapped his arms around his son, told him again there was no need to be sorry, and what I heard was anger. What I heard was the indignation of a good man railing against the hours he'd spent beating himself up over not having spoken up or being too loyal, over being nothing more than good old Jim, a trombonist in a well-reputed orchestra, a good father and colleague, a good husband and neighbour, who had cultivated humility and a sense of responsibility throughout his life, *Christ, since childhood*, and had reaped the honorable fruit, he loved, he loved, *I love you, Tessa, I love you so much*, but every morning he continued to wake up with a ball of fear in his gut and an irrepressible urge to apologize. *That Jim no longer existed.*

Father and son continued to surrender to the rapture of tears and now, in the bar, looking at Francis's hands, hands so clean they seem to be gloves, his nails white from holding the bottle so tight, everything becomes perfectly clear.

My words materialize of their own accord: "I don't think so, no. I'll be leaving soon."

Francis doesn't insist. In fact, I suspect he's relieved. His fingers loosen their grip on the bottle, and he hurries off to pay.

"My treat, it's the least I can do."

The least, yes, not that that changes anything; Anthony already said it was his treat. I head for the washroom. Sitting in the cubicle with its twenty years' worth of graffiti, my eyes locked on my golden ballerina flats and my hiked-up dress, I give a strangled chirp, the cry of a startled bird. *How about that. What a good story I'll have for Sophie.* I carefully wash my hands, the bubblegum scent of the soap both repels and attracts me. A glance in the mirror, but a fleeting glance, nothing more. I no longer care what Francis sees when he looks at me.

He's already outside. I walk through the bar and give Anthony a wave. Does he think we're in a hurry to hole up in a hotel room together somewhere? I don't care about that either. Did Francis even book a room? I won't ask. Of course, I'd be flattered. But nothing more.

I PUSH ON THE door and step outside. Francis turns to me, a light spring breeze riffling his hair and, for the space of an instant, he looks as young as that day I first saw him on the work site in Ottawa. *But nothing more.*

"Can I drop you off?"

"No, I'll walk."

"All the way to Villeray?"

"It's no big deal."

Our hug is brief and weary. I've imagined for days — actually, for years, to be honest — that we'd cleave together from the first second on, that our fingers would seek each other out, that there'd be no resistance possible once in his arms, the affair would play itself out as only it knew how, there'd be no going back, the fever on the phone, hands trembling as I swam, my sobs between the sheets. That's what I expected. In his awkward hug, like some Lego block you're struggling to fit into one of another make, all I can feel is Francis's slippery jacket and the scent of melted ice on his scarf.

"So long, Marianne."

I smile, not showing any teeth.

"We'll call?"

I nod because we may well call each other, I'm selling his house after all, but even as I nod, my eyes say *See you never, alligator,* and he knows it, and I know it, and sometimes that's the way love affairs end, even the most stubborn of them all.

My first sale was a dilapidated duplex converted into condos on Drolet at Faillon. Nothing too ambitious. Two old apartments that had been remodeled to make three units. The people selling, a musician couple from the orchestra, had bought the building a year earlier to have it renovated. I'd got my licence two months before that and had just joined the ranks of a brokerage franchise. Our friends burst out laughing when I announced my plans. They pounded their thighs when I told them about the training I'd go through and rolled around on the floor when I dithered out loud between one banner and another. *Give us a break! You're going back to university at last, right?* But I did take the courses and passed the final with flying colours. From that day on, they stopped laughing and only broached the subject, embarrassed and overly polite, as though I were some distant relative they felt they couldn't ignore. No one ever spoke of music with me again. But Jim never laughed. He just said, "How about we hook up secretly in the empty apartments?"

When he heard some colleagues were looking to sell their unit, he saw the perfect opportunity; the building was in our neighbourhood in a promising market. Philémon was five; Boris had just turned three. I had stayed at home with them since they were born. The time had come to get back in the saddle. No matter which saddle, or what it should have been or never would be.

They showed me pictures of the original duplex. It was lopsided and fascinating, with its art deco bathroom (honeycomb ceramic tile, clawfoot bathtub, built-in soap dish) and its central gas furnace (a rarity that was also quite impractical). Stéphane and Josée had hired an unscrupulous contractor who had demolished the building and erected in its stead a beige brick box flanked by white PVC stairs and grey PVC windows. The result was appalling, but square. The old double rooms had been replaced by reasonably sized and aligned bedrooms. Prefabricated cabinets replaced the old kitchen cupboards so the indispensable open concept area could work its magic on potential buyers. *Together time! Intimacy! Glasses of wine by the fireside!* The living rooms had no fireplace, that would have been too expensive, and the city would have kicked up a fuss. But the contractor said an actual fire didn't matter; you just needed to get the same feeling. He knew what he was talking about. The other two units sold in a few short weeks.

After a year in their renovated building, Stéphane and Josée separated. Whether their desire frayed or the bathroom's textured tiles spoiled it for them, I never knew. When they toured the apartment with me, they gave nothing away. They laughed remembering the catastrophic day a worker drilled a hole in the wall and straight into the new drainpipe installed just the week before; they tapped each other on the shoulder gently to tweak the other's anecdote or memory. The morning of the first open house, Josée insisted on baking cookies since she'd read somewhere that it would make the apartment seem more appealing (they've all read that somewhere). Stéphane scarfed down all the cookies before the first visitors arrived, leaving an empty plate on the kitchen island. Josée wasn't upset. She laughed, "Stéphane has a sweet tooth." I remember thinking, *Why on earth are they separating?*

The condo sold in forty-six days, earning me kudos from my new colleagues and a solid reputation with the orchestra. Josée and Stéphane were thrilled; separately, they asked me to help them find new apartments. Last year, the unit sold again. Another separation.

As I walk past the building tonight with Oscar's hand in mine — formerly I'd thought that it would be Jim who'd get him, that I'd send a hasty message in between sessions of infinitely joyous lovemaking, something like, *Can't come home yet, could you pick up Oscar, I'll keep you posted* — I notice that the new owners have changed the windows. They're black now, the tilt-and-turn kind, and the new railing to the stairs is in wrought iron, black as well, as it used to be in the original building. They have planted tulips and lilies of the valley in the small patch of earth beside the building.

Through a half-open door, I can see that the new owners have also transformed the whole apartment. Now there's only one closed-off room; the rest is an open floorplan, and you can see through to the back wall itself, one big window. Strands of lights zigzag above the backyard. A breeze penetrates the apartment and sets the planter hung on the front balcony to swaying.

The clawfoot bathtub is long gone. And the waterfall shower is said to be stunning with its brass fittings, just like the ones in magazines.

"French expats, so in love," I'm told by Julien, the server from the café, who knows everything.

Acknowledgements

The author would like to thank the Canada Council for the Arts for its financial support, which made the completion of this project possible.

Thanks go out to Élisabeth Comtois and Émilie Laforest for their valuable knowledge of the world of music, and to Armande Ouellet for her research on Abitibi.

Thanks to Samuel Lambert, first reader and first refuge.

Thanks to Kelly Joseph, Amelia Spedaliere, and the whole team at House of Anansi for welcoming Tessa into their home, and to the wonderful Susan Ouriou and Christelle Morelli for uncovering her English voice.

Lastly, thanks to Geneviève Thibault, reader, editor, and exceptional woman; if this book is in some small way of worth, it will be in large part through her doing.

About the Author

FANNY BRITT is a writer, playwright, and translator. She has written a dozen plays and translated more than fifteen. She is the winner of the 2013 Governor General's Literary Award for Drama for her play *Bienveillance.* *Jane, the Fox and Me,* her first graphic novel, was a finalist for the Governor General's Literary Award for Children's Literature — Text; was the winner of a Libris Award and a Joe Shuster award; and was on the *New York Times* Best Illustrated Books list. Her debut novel *Les Maisons* (*Hunting Houses*), was a finalist for the Prix littéraire des collégiens and the Prix littéraire France-Québec.

About the Translators

SUSAN OURIOU is an award-winning writer and literary translator working from French and Spanish into English with more than thirty literary translations to her credit. She has won the Governor General's Literary Award for Translation and been part of the Banff International Literary Translation Centre since its creation.

CHRISTELLE MORELLI is a literary translator and French immersion teacher. She has translated several works of fiction for publication, including *Jane, the Fox and Me* and *Stolen Sisters*, a finalist for the Governor General's Literary Award for Translation. Having lived in Quebec and France, she now makes her home with her family in Western Canada.